THE
BOOK
OF
ABISH

BY COMMON CONSENT PRESS is a non-profit publisher dedicated to producing affordable, high-quality books that help define and shape the Latter-day Saint experience. BCC Press publishes books that address all aspects of Mormon life. Our mission includes finding manuscripts that will contribute to the lives of thoughtful Latter-day Saints, mentoring authors and nurturing projects to completion, and distributing important books to the Mormon audience at the lowest possible cost.

THE
BOOK
OF
ABISH

Mette Harrison

`

For information contact
By Common Consent Press
4062 S. Evelyn Dr.
Salt Lake City, UT 84124-2250

Cover design: D Christian Harrison
Book design: Andrew Heiss

www.bccpress.org

ISBN-10: 1-948218-08-9
ISBN-13: 978-1-948218-08-5

10 9 8 7 6 5 4 3 2 1

To my daughters, who keep complaining that I haven't dedicated a book to them yet:

Hope
Sage
Faith

(As for my sons—you get none! Yet.)

Foreword
by
Michael Austin

And it came to pass that they did call on the name of the Lord, in their might, even until they had all fallen to the earth, save it were one of the Lamanitish women, whose name was Abish, she having been converted unto the Lord for many years, on account of a remarkable vision of her father—

Thus, having been converted to the Lord, and never having made it known, therefore, when she saw that all the servants of Lamoni had fallen to the earth, and also her mistress, the queen, and the king, and Ammon lay prostrate upon the earth, she knew that it was the power of God; and supposing that this opportunity, by making known unto the people what had happened among them, that by beholding this scene it would cause them to believe in the power of God, therefore she ran forth from house to house, making it known unto the people.

—Alma 19:16–17

This is all that we are told about the Lamanite woman named Abish in the Book of Mormon: her father had a vision from the Lord, she was herself converted as a consequence of this vision, she recognizes what is happening when Lamoni and every other member of his household falls to the earth in a trance-like state, and she tells everybody what is really going on. In this way, she brings about the conversion, and the salvation, of her people.

It is a remarkable—and remarkably incomplete story for one of the only three women named in the Book of Mormon. The other two are easier to interpret. Sariah was the wife of Lehi, the mother of Laman, Lemuel, Nephi, and Sam, and the matriarch of all of the peoples described in the Book of Mormon. Isabel was a harlot who tempted the prophet's kid and caused him to fall into sexual temptation. Both women are different sides of the same sexualized female archetype—the mother and the whore. We understand why they are in the story.

But Abish is something else entirely. She is not a stock character, but a vital mover of one of the most important events in the Book of Mormon: the mass conversion of the Lamanites to the One True God of the Nephites. She is more responsible than any other character for breaking down the organizing dichotomies of the story: Nephites are white, delightsome, and good; Lamanites are dark, not particularly delightsome, and bad.

Until Abish comes along. Here we have a Lamanite woman who is good and brave. She has somehow found her way to the True God without the help of any Nephites, and she plays an important ecclesiastical role that does not require the permission of any man. Where did such a woman come from? Why do we only get two verses about her in the Book of Mormon? How can we make the silence in the text speak to us?

This, it turns out, is what really good writers do. They put clothes on the skeletal fragments that we see in scriptural texts. They create fictional stories that help us see deeper truths. They make the silences speak.

And Mette Harrison is a really good writer.

In the publication sequence, *The Book of Abish* is a sequel to Harrison's 2017 novel, *The Book of Laman*. But the two volumes are not connected in any but the broadest terms—they are both novels based on Book of Mormon characters. *The Book of Abish* stands on its own as a deep re-imagining of the story of Ammon's mission to the Lamanites in Alma 18–19. Harrison gives Abish a history, a personality, and a set of experiences with the divine that explains how she managed to be in King Lamoni's palace when Ammon arrived from Zarahemla with the gospel.

Abish's story is compelling in its own right. She is born the seventh daughter of a wealthy man, who has no son to carry on his affairs. When he dies, his family becomes desperately poor, but he tells Abish about the vision he had when she was born, and it changes her life forever. Sort of. But not really.

What changes her life forever is her own experience with the One True God. After she promises her father that she will pray to him, she does. And he speaks back:

> *With that, Abish felt as if she had been washed clean, and that all of her fears and worries about her father, her mother and sisters, her mortal life, were gone. She felt a warmth inside of her heart that she had never known before. She knew that this One True God loved her more deeply than she could comprehend and that nothing she did or did not do would ever separate them again. (62)*

Abish, in other words, must learn to trust her own spiritual experiences. And she must trust that the God she believes in loves her, has always love her, and will love her more deeply than she could comprehend, and that there is nothing that she could ever do to change that love.

This is the balm that the *Book of Abish* brings to us: the powerful testimony of a deeply spiritual writer that we can trust our own spiritual experiences and that the True God loves us absolutely and unconditionally. Nothing matters as much as this does. And nothing can ever change it.

And when Ammon brings the word of the Nephite God to the Lamanite court, this is the experience that Abish recalls. And this is the message she wants to share with her king, her family, and her people. God loves you. God will talk to you. You are enough, and you don't need Nephites, or kings, or fathers, churches, or men, or anybody else to tell you this because you can trust your own spiritual experiences.

And when the time is right, you can change your world.

Prologue

When Timah saw that she had given birth to a seventh girl, she was afraid. Her husband had been disappointed that his first child had been a daughter, and he had been more and more disappointed with each subsequent daughter born. When Timah had delivered her sixth daughter, he had accused her of being a witch.

He had said, "You have made some great sacrifice to the evil one to ensure that I have no sons to come after me. If you bring another daughter to me, I will kill her and then I will kill you and all the others. I will know then that it is true what the others say, that they are not my children, but the children of the one who wears a single horn and lives inside the earth."

Timah had never made a bargain with the evil one. She knew of other women who made sacrifices to him, some who had even begged for a daughter after many sons, some who pleaded for release from a husband who abused them, some who asked for riches. But she had never seen the horned one, and she had no interest in being released from her marriage.

She loved Haman. He was a brick builder and he worked hard for their family. He did not drink wine, and she was sure he had been faithful to her during their marriage. He treated their daughters with kindness and respect. He even took the older ones with him from time to time and taught them what he knew of his trade. He was a good husband, and she suspected that his angry words had been aroused by his brothers, who were coarse men and who did not treat their wives or their daughters kindly.

But still, she was afraid. He had spoken the words in public, where his brothers had heard him. They would try to hold him to his oath. She had to make sure that he saw his daughter himself before he heard the news. He would see then how beautiful the new little girl was and how much she looked like him. All the girls had looked like their father when they were first born. They all had his nose and his brow. This little one had his jawline, as well. She was already strong, and she would grow stronger still—if she was given a chance.

But he would be disappointed because Timah was too old to have another child, and his hope for a son from her would have to be given up. If he spoke to his brothers, they would stir up his anger. He would forget that his daughters were his most beloved possessions and that he loved his wife. He would think about the stories of the evil one lying with Timah.

She put the baby to her breast immediately, so that the little girl would not cry out. She seemed to know exactly what to do and was sucking happily, her little arm reaching for her mother. Timah gave her daughter her finger to hold onto. The grip was tight.

What to name her? The other girls had been named after men in Haman's family, to make them happier about the lack of sons, but this time, Timah wanted to name the little girl herself.

After her mother?

No.

Timah's mother had died when Timah was very young and she hardly remembered her.

This baby seemed to be her own person and deserved her own unique name.

She had thick, dark hair curling around her ears. She was long and dark-skinned, sturdy, and bright-eyed.

"I love you, little one. But you know that, don't you?" Timah whispered to her daughter.

The baby looked up at her mother, and Timah felt a shiver run through her. She knew this girl. She had met her before. She did not know where, but it was one of those moments the shamans talked about, a glimpse into the other world, beyond this one of flesh and bone. The higher world where the gods dwelled. Abish had just come from that place, and she must have carried some of it with her to touch Timah.

"Were we sisters there?" Timah said softly. "Or were you my guiding light?" She tried these out, but neither of them seemed right. "Or were you my daughter there as well?" she asked.

Yes, that seemed right. They had been mother and child in the other world. Perhaps it had been true for her other daughters too, but Timah had never felt so sure of it as she was in this moment with this baby. She knew that this was the child who was supposed to come. There was something special in her, something that the whole family needed. She was fated to come to them and to do some important work.

"If we can keep you alive," Timah said. "Then we will all find out what that is, won't we?" She smoothed the baby's hair, and with that, the name came to her.

Abish.

It was as if her daughter had spoken the sounds to her, though she had not heard anything.

"Little Abish, with so much work to do already. Did the Great One send you to us with starlight trailing after you?" The father of all the Gods was not often heard from on earth. He had many other worlds to rule over, and that was why He sent the younger gods to care for His children here, the gods of earth and fire and water. The gods of trees, and His shaman, who spoke for Him when they were in a trance.

Timah had meant to stay awake, but the next thing she knew, she was startled awake by the sound of the door opening and the sight of her husband coming into the room.

"I was afraid that you had died," he said gently. The expression on his face was so soft that she let herself forget for a moment what he had threatened.

"I'm well," she said.

"And the babe?" he asked.

She held the tightly wrapped bundle up.

"I will call her Abish," she said.

She meant to say more, to tell Haman about the feeling she had experienced, that this child was sent from the Great One, and that she had a work to do. But Haman had stopped very still, his body turned to stone.

"Her?" he said. "It is another girl?"

Timah glanced at the door. There was no way she could get to it without having to pass Haman by. She would give her life for her daughter, for any of her daughters, but the youngest was the most vulnerable. How could she save Abish?

"Haman, I know you are a good man. I know that you love me," she said softly.

"It is impossible that a man could have seven daughters in a row without witchcraft," he said.

4

"I made no bargains with the evil one, Haman, I swear." She was beginning to be truly afraid. Haman's face had gone red with anger, and his hands were clenched. His brothers were not even here to press him to follow through on his oath. Were they waiting outside? Had they waited until this moment to remind him of his oath before he came into his wife.

"She is yours. See?" Timah held the baby up. "She has your nose, like the other girls."

But Haman was in no mood to hear this. He strode forward swiftly, yanked the babe out of Timah's hands before she could think of what to do, and held her too high for Timah to get to her, even if she had been strong enough after childbirth. Haman was a huge man. His years of brick-building had made him twice her size.

"Please, let her go. Please, I beg you. She is innocent. She has done nothing. If you are angry, Haman, be angry with me. It is my fault that you have seven daughters and no sons. Strike me if you must, or kill me. But let your daughter live."

She knelt down before Haman, tears streaming down her face. All she could do now was beg for her daughter. Nobody was to blame for any of this. A woman who had sons was told she was honored of the gods, but what did she do right or wrong? Nothing. It was what the gods chose, not what she had chosen.

Haman had dislodged the blanket around the baby and was swinging her around by her legs. But little Abish did not cry. She was alert, awake, and she seemed to know her father as she had known her mother.

"Great God of All, protect her," Timah prayed silently, her lips moving, though she dared not speak the words aloud while Haman was here.

She could not bear to see what would happen next, so she closed her eyes.

She did not see Haman fall to the ground, but she heard the heavy thump of his body hitting the floor. At first she thought that it was the sound of Haman throwing himself to the ground to crush his daughter in his arms.

But when she dared to open her eyes, she saw little Abish lying on top of her father, whose eyes were closed and whose body was very still.

Whatever had happened, there was no mark on him. Had the Great One struck him down in punishment for his oath? Did the Great One love Abish so much? Timah was even more in awe of her young daughter than she had been before.

She inched forward, fearful of disturbing Haman, then reached for Abish and pulled her close to her breast once more. She found the blanket and wrapped that around her as well. The baby had not uttered a cry, nor shown any sign of distress. That seemed as much a miracle to Timah as Hamar's silent fall.

"Thank you for saving my child. I promise you that I will raise her to know you. She will worship only you," Timah prayed again, rocking Abish back and forth, tears streaming down her face.

"Mama?" said a familiar voice some time later. "Is the baby born?"

Timah looked up and saw that it was Tamar, the oldest of her daughters, now twelve years of age. She was taller than Timah and was proud of the fact that she seemed to be on track to gain her father's height.

"There she is. Can I hold her?" said Tamar, coming to a stop when she saw her father's body on the ground. "What happened to Father?" she asked.

"I don't know," Timah said honestly. "He fell to the ground."

Tamar looked at her mother with fear for a long moment. Did she think that there was witchcraft involved in this as well?

"Come, take your sister and I will try to wake your father," Timah said, holding out the baby. Then the baby would be safe, at least.

Tamar did as she was bid, and then Timah spent hours trying to wake her husband. She threw cold water over him. She pinched his face. She slapped his cheeks. She tried yelling at him. She begged the Great One to wake him. She did not dare to call to the evil, horned one though. Nor did she send for the shaman. She was terrified of what would happen if Haman's brothers heard what had happened to him. But how many days could she wait before rumors began and others came to accuse her of witchcraft?

On the third day, Timah woke in her bed and saw that Haman had moved. Or had he? Was it just her hope?

"Haman?" she said softly. "Haman, are you there?"

He stirred, though his eyes were still closed.

He was not dead, then! Tamar had said that she thought her father had begun to stink, but Timah did not think so.

"Haman, wake up. Come see your daughter." She hoped that by now he would have forgotten his foolish oath and that he might feel weak enough not to threaten any physical harm on his child again—or on her.

Indeed, Haman opened his eyes and moved very slowly. "What happened?" he asked, his words slurred.

"You fell to the ground," Timah said. "It must have been the power of the Great One at work. I was telling you that the new baby, Abish, was a special spirit that had been sent to us." She did not want to remind him of what his reaction had been.

"I saw a vision," Haman said, lifting his head from the ground.

"What?"

"The Great One came to me and spoke to me. He told me that He was the Father of us all, that His Son would come into the world as the Nephites have been telling us for many years. He told me that Abish would be the one to convert my brothers and all my family and all our village and even our kingdom to the truth. He told me that I must protect her, for she was called to this from before her birth."

Now Timah stared at her husband. She had never expected that he would have a vision, but this was an answer to her prayer to the Great One. She had heard nothing about the Nephites, but as her husband spoke, she felt a return of that warm shivering feeling she'd felt at the name she'd given her daughter. Perhaps the Nephite one God was not so far from her old belief in the Great One.

"That is good," she said. "That is also what I believe." And as she spoke it, she realized it was true. How was it so easy to accept what should have been heresy? If either she or Haman spoke these words outside of this room, they would be killed for treachery to the Lamanite king, as was anyone who preached Nephite doctrines of God.

"We must not speak of this until the right time. We must wait for Abish to understand who she is," Haman said, looking deeply into his wife's eyes. There was a plea for forgiveness in there, but it seemed unimportant compared to all else that had come to them.

Timah reached for his hand. "We will keep her safe," she said. "No matter what your brothers say."

"My brothers," Haman said, as he rose unsteadily to his feet, his arm catching her. He leaned on her for the first time in their life together as she helped him to the bed.

"You need food," she said. She did not want to press him about his brothers.

"My brothers are fools," he said. "I will never allow them to step foot in this house again, Timah. I promise you that."

And it was a promise he kept all the rest of his days.

1

As a young child, Abish felt guilty sometimes that she was her father's favorite. All of her sisters knew it. No one pretended anything different. When he came home from work, her father put Abish on his shoulders and carried her around, boasting that she was so tall that she could reach the clouds. He bought her special gifts for no reason at all. A beautiful dress with pearls sewn onto the hem and the collar, a necklace made with precious stones that exactly matched her dark eyes, a piece of silk to wrap around her neck, though none of her sisters wore any such thing.

One day, her father announced that Abish was the "queen of his heart," and so instead of going to work, he would build her a proper castle, as she deserved. It would have many of the features of the king's own home, which her father had helped to build years ago. It was as tall as he was and as wide around as his arms could reach, but inside there was a secret space under the floor with a trap door that opened into it. It was too small for any of her sisters to fit inside, but Abish would sometimes hide away in that special place for hours just to annoy her sisters who were looking for her.

It wasn't until she was much older that Abish realized that her oldest sister Tamar had been the favorite before her. She used to go with her father to work often and she still tried to get him to talk to her whenever he came home. Yet Haman seemed to only see Abish.

Abish began to wonder if her father's treatment would change, if he would turn his favor to someone else.

"When will you have another baby?" she asked her mother one day.

"What?" Her mother looked up at her from kneading bread. "What makes you ask a question like that, Abish?"

"Because if you have another girl, Father will love her more than he loves me." It only occurred to Abish as she spoke that it might be even worse if her mother had a son. She'd seen other fathers with their sons in the marketplace. They ignored their daughters completely.

"Well, you don't have to worry about that because I'm too old to have more children," said her mother, leaning in and kissing Abish on the nose. "And besides, I don't think it's possible for any man to love a daughter more than your father loves you."

"But what about a son? Doesn't Father want a son?" Abish asked.

"He did want a son, yes, but now he has you and he is as happy as any man could ever be."

Abish didn't argue with her mother, but she continued to watch carefully when she saw other men with their sons in the marketplace. It seemed clear that all fathers preferred sons.

One day she slipped away from her mother while she was looking at clothing and found one of the men she had seen with his son, laughing with him, thumping him on the back. The boy was about Abish's own age, though Abish did not know either of them.

"Excuse me," she said.

"What is it? Are you selling something?" the man asked.

"No. I wanted to ask a question," she said. "About your son?"

The man nudged his son and whispered something to him that Abish could not hear. The two laughed together, and Abish felt uncomfortable with the way they looked at her.

"Well, go on," the man urged her. "Ask your question. You want to know if you will marry my son when he is older, don't you? He is handsome and strong and you want him for yourself. But I see no reason to make promises when he will soon have the pick of every woman in the kingdom, even the king's own daughter, if he wishes."

Abish had not meant to ask anything of the sort. She hadn't thought of marriage for herself, though she knew some of her older sisters spoke about it. "I—" she began, and stopped.

"If you cannot even speak, how do you think you will get any man to want you? Unless you are wealthy enough that they do not care if you have a brain in your head," the man said. Then he squinted at her. "Wait a moment—you are Haman's daughter, aren't you? The youngest one he makes such a fuss over. But you are not even pretty. Why does your father think you are so precious?"

This was the first time in her life that Abish had been told any such thing. Her father told her she was the most beautiful girl in the world, that she would grow up to be the most beautiful woman. He told her that she was so beautiful the stars in the sky were envious of her, and that the sun slipped away into the mountains each evening because it was tired of trying to outshine her.

"My father thinks I'm beautiful," Abish said, though the words were hard to speak. Her chest felt heavy and she wanted desperately to run away. But her father wouldn't want her to do that. He expected Abish to be brave as well as beautiful.

"Does he? Or does he tell you that because he is ashamed that he has only daughters instead of sons? If he had seven sons instead of seven daughters, I think that he would not need to worry so much about the future of his business. He would already be able to retire and live in peace and wealth. But because he has daughters, he must work until his dying day." The man waved at Abish in dismissal and turned to walk away with his son.

"Wait!" Abish called out.

He turned back to face her, his expression dour. "What?"

"Why do fathers love sons so much more than daughters?" she asked. It wasn't quite what she'd meant to say, but the man had already told her a lot.

"Because a man can talk to his son in a way he can never talk to his wife or his daughters. They will never understand him."

"But a daughter can listen," Abish said.

The man sneered. "A daughter can listen. But she can never understand what it is to be a man. A daughter will always be second-best. I'm sure your father loves you. I love my daughter as well. But it is not the same. Daughters are for a mother. They will keep her happy in her old age. But for a man, a son is the only way to the future." He walked away from her, and Abish wished she had never spoken to him.

She told herself that he was lying, that he was cruel and small-minded and that her father was far above him. She turned to try to find her mother in the marketplace ,and it took her a few minutes to get her bearings. Everything seemed different than it had been before, darker and colder. But she backtracked and found her mother at the same clothing stall where she had left her only a little while before. Abish's heart was so heavy, but she did not explain to her mother why.

"What about this? You would look lovely in this." Her mother held up a swatch of bright blue fabric to Abish's face. "Your father would love you in that."

Abish batted it away. "I don't want it," she said stubbornly.

Her mother seemed confused. "All right. What about this, then?" She held up a brilliant red.

"No," Abish said. "I don't want new clothes."

"But I thought you said you did this morning. You said that everything around your chest is too small."

"I don't care. My old things are better than any of this," Abish said. She made a face at the stall owner and he looked hurt.

"My fabric is the best in the market and my daughters and I are superb with a needle," he insisted.

He had daughters, not sons, thought Abish. Did he wish for sons, too?

They walked away from the clothing stall and Abish's mother chastised her for her rudeness. "Your father tells you you are a princess, but that does not give you the right to treat other people as your servants."

"You don't love me. You've never loved me!" Abish accused her mother.

"Never loved you! You foolish, selfish girl. I loved you first. I saved you from your father, who might have killed you when you were born but for me. The seventh daughter. He threatened me that he would kill you and me, as well, if you were not a son."

Abish cried out at this, and turned to look at her mother, sure that she would see that her mother had lied to her. But no, that was truth on her face, and the stricken look proved it.

Abish ran from her, all the way home, despite her mother's calls after her. She hid herself in her tiny secret room in her castle and stayed there until her father returned home from his work that evening.

He knocked on her door. "Abish? Abish, come and talk to me. Your mother says that you have had a terrible day."

Had her mother told her father what she'd said about her birth? Abish couldn't believe it. She didn't want to believe it. How could her father, who loved her so much, have ever threatened such a thing? How could she ever feel safe with him again if he had said he would kill her and her mother?

But she came out of the secret space. The truth was, she was getting too big for it, and she was tired of being cramped and dark and alone. She forced her legs to straighten and climbed out to face her father.

"You've been crying. Why is that?" Her father wiped at her face.

"Do you wish you had a son instead of me?" Abish asked bluntly.

"What makes you ask that? Have I not told you how much I love you enough in the last week?" said her father, smiling gently. "Do you not remember how I carry you on my head through the marketplace to show everyone my beautiful daughter?"

"Don't call me that," Abish said.

"My beautiful daughter? But you are beautiful and you are my daughter," her father insisted.

"The man in the market today said that I'm not beautiful. He said that you pretend that because you have no sons. But that all men wish for sons because they cannot talk to daughters, and daughters will never be men."

Her father laughed. "I am talking to you right now!" he said and grinned at her.

"This is not a joke, Father," Abish said. "Mother told me that you threatened to kill her if she did not have a son."

Her father's face changed. He looked away from her, ashamed. "I wish she had not told you that."

It was true, then. Abish felt sick. Her father was a liar. He did not love her like a princess. He'd wanted a son all along. He still wanted a son.

He let out a long breath. "I did not understand the truth. I thought that what mattered in this life was having a son to carry on your business and to laugh with you about things men laugh about. I thought—it was an affront to my manhood that my wife could make me no sons. I worried that other men were mocking me when I could not hear them."

This did not sound like her father at all. Whoever this man was he was talking about, Abish was glad that she had never known him.

"Mother says that she is too old to have more children," Abish said.

Her father bowed his head. "Yes, I believe that is true."

"Then why don't you put her away, and all of her daughters, and marry a younger woman who can give you sons? You have money enough for that. Your business is very successful. And then you could have the sons you wanted." It was the worst thing Abish could imagine, and so she forced herself to imagine it.

"But I don't want another wife. I don't want to put my daughters away. I love them. And I love you most of all, Abish." Her father's face was pale, as if this was the worst thing he could imagine too.

"Are you sure?" Abish asked.

Her father held out his arms and pressed her to his chest. "I'm very sure, Princess. I could not imagine any son in the world who could make me as happy as you do."

Abish considered for a little while, then pulled away from her father. "Then why do other fathers want sons so much? Why not daughters?"

"Because they are foolish men and cannot see the truth that is right in front of their faces and the joy that their daughters would bring them if only they understood."

There was something else her father was not telling her, Abish realized. But it was not a bad thing. She would let it go for now. She was happy enough to be told that she was still her father's princess, even if she was growing too big for her secret space. Her father would build her something else if she wanted. But for now, she said, "Will you take me to the market and buy me clothes?"

She held her breath for a moment, waiting for her father to say that it was beneath him, that it was her mother's job, that it was woman's work. But he didn't. He held out a hand for her and said, "let's go tell your mother," and that was that.

2

In her early years, Abish always had the finest clothing to wear as well as jewelry that no other child had. Her sisters complained sometimes that their father didn't give them such prizes, and then their father would bring home something for everyone, a precious stone for each sister to wear on a chain or a feather for each of them to put in their hair. But always there was something extra for Abish.

"Because you are my princess," he said, and kissed her lightly before going back to the others and pretending that he loved them just as much.

Abish knew that her sisters did not think of her as one of them. They had more chores to do around the house than she did. The oldest two girls, Tamar and Nesha, both had jobs they worked outside the home to earn money for themselves. They bought themselves what they wanted and seemed proud of their independence. But they could never afford the kinds of things that their father bought for Abish. They did not have his wealth or his connections. He found things that were not available in the marketplace, original items that no one else could buy.

Abish was used to spending time with her mother, going to the marketplace and doing chores around the house, but her father had begun to hire servants to do these tasks instead.

Her mother complained, "Your father hires servants for his own status, not because I asked him for them. They are heavy ornaments to carry around, when you are used to lifting your own weight."

There were servants to clean the house, as well as to cook, and this meant that Abish spent more time alone. She had plenty of toys her father had gifted to her, but she had become tired of toys and baubles. She wanted to talk to other children, but when she went outside her house, no one would speak to her. The neighbor children often scattered from her, laughing as if it were some game. But sometimes they refused to move and stared at her mulishly, waiting for her to leave.

"It's not fair," Abish complained to her father when he came home from dinner that night, as she and her father sat in the quiet feeling of having eaten enough food that they would not feel hungry again for some time. "Why won't they be friends with me?"

"Do you want me to buy you friends as I buy your mother servants?" her father asked.

Abish was not sure for a long moment whether her father was serious or not. Was the answer so simple? Could her father buy friends for her?

"No," she said slowly, "I don't want that."

"Then what? Shall I threaten them? Tell them that their fathers will not be allowed to work with me if the children are not your friends?" He raised his eyebrows at her.

"No," Abish said again, ashamed of the suggestion.

"Then what do you think you can do to make friends of them?"

"I don't know," Abish said impatiently. She'd spent months trying to figure this out. She'd done everything she could. "I bring my toys out and offer to share them." What more could they want?

"And they don't appreciate it?" her father asked.

"They laugh and call me 'princess' and run away."

"Do you treat them as servants? Do you demand they play as you say with your toys?" asked her father.

Abish was not sure how to answer this. "They are my toys," she said.

"Ah. And you have never considered giving the toys away? Not even the ones that you no longer play with?"

"But you gave them to me. They're mine," Abish said. It had never occurred to her until that moment that as the youngest daughter, she'd never had to offer her old toys to a younger child the way that all her sisters must have done. But they had not had as many as she had. It must have been easier for them to share than it was for her.

"Abish, you are too old to be so selfish. Do you think you will never have to share anything in your life? When you marry and have children of your own, you will need to learn to share. Your house. Your bed. Your food. Everything will be shared. Sharing is the way to joy and happiness, not keeping things to yourself," her father said gently.

She felt a fire of fury growing in her heart. Why was her father telling her this now? "I thought I was to be a prin-cess. I thought you would build me a castle of my own, and I would never have to share anything because you would give me all that I wanted."

Her father stared at her as though he were seeing her for the first time—and he did not like what he saw. "Abish, my sweet daughter, I have always treasured you as a glow-ing gemstone, and I built you a little castle of your own so that you would feel special. But tell me honestly that you

20

would not want to live in such a place alone forever just so that you would not have to share with anyone?"

It was clear that he felt disappointed in her, but it wasn't fair. He'd never demanded that she share anything before. He'd always told the other girls not to be jealous of her, to leave her alone, that she was the baby. He'd defended her.

What had happened to the father she thought of as her king? "I don't see what is wrong with wanting to be special," she said defiantly.

"Your mother is special, but she gives all she has to her daughters. Do you not see how that makes her happy?" her father demanded.

But she wasn't her mother, and she didn't want to be. She wanted to be a princess in truth as well as in her father's eyes. "I don't want to share," she said stubbornly.

Her father put his thick, heavy hands on her shoulders and twisted her around until she could not avoid meeting his eyes. "Abish, I have spoiled you. I can see that now. I should never have called you my 'princess.' Not if it turned you into a selfish girl. You will never be happy if you don't learn to share. Those children are jealous of you. They want to be your friends, but they're afraid that you look down on them. You have to show them that you do not."

Abish let tears spill from her eyes. She had always cried easily, but this time she did not even try to stop the tears. She wanted her father to see how hurt she was. He'd always done whatever she asked when she cried before.

But his mouth tightened instead of relaxing and he said, "No, Abish. I don't care if you cry this time. I want you to promise me that you will share. Tomorrow. You will take your toys into the street and share them with the other children. Do you hear me?"

His fingers gripped her shoulders tightly. This was the first time he had ever shown disapproval to her, and it only made her angry.

"I don't want to," she said.

His grip tightened. "Tell me you will, Abish. I will come home tomorrow and ask if you have done it, and if you have not . . ." there was a long pause as Abish realized that her father was thinking of a punishment, even for his princess.

Then he finished with, "I will send you into your castle without any toys at all, and without any food, for a day, until you come to me and tell me that you will do as I have commanded you. I am your father, and you must obey me."

She hated this father. Where had her true father gone? She wanted him back. Abish locked her jaw, convinced that she could outlast her father's anger. He must have had a bad day and forgotten that she was his princess. But tomorrow he would. Surely, he would.

Her father let her go and she thought that was the end of it. He smiled and teased her at dinner and he tucked her into her voluminous bed that night, a bed twice as big as her parents' bed was, and filled with downy pillows and blankets.

But in the morning, before he left for work, he looked across to her and said, "Remember, Abish. You are to share today."

There was a tone in his voice that made her afraid of him. Her father had never lied to her before, and so she was sure that he would come home and ask her if she'd done what he said.

Fine, then, she would. She would bring out all the toys that she had outgrown, all the toys that she no longer played with, the ones that she did not care about. She could share those with the dirty, stupid, mean children on the street. Let them have all of them.

She began to cart out armfuls of toys from her castle, from her bedroom, from the trunks where they were held all over the house, from the floors, from the corners of rooms she had forgotten that she had even left toys in. She threw everything in a pile and could see the other children stare at her, watching her, half-afraid of what she was doing. They whispered and waited until she was finished, and then she stood over everything, her arms folded across her chest.

"Come out and play with them!" she called out.

But they didn't come. They didn't even look at her or her toys. They weren't jealous of her. They didn't want to make friends if she would only give them a chance. And she didn't care anyway. She didn't want to be friends with them either. Not if they looked at her like that.

She was so angry that she began to throw the toys at the rocks on the side of the street, trying to break them. She wanted nothing left of these stupid toys that had led her to her argument with her father and his complete change in attitude toward her. If she had to choose between toys and being her father's princess, she knew which one she would choose.

The children backed away from her as bits and pieces of her toys flew into the air. Abish was soon covered in tiny cuts that bled on her face, her arms, and her legs.

One of the children ran forward between her throwing toys and grabbed her hands. "Stop it! You useless idiot! Why do you have to ruin everything for everybody?"

She stared at him and yanked her arms away. "Why do you hate me?" she asked.

"Because you've never bothered to know any of us, Princess," he said. "You think you are better than we are, with all your toys and your lonely little castle."

She could have said something friendly. She could have asked him to share a toy with her, or to come back to her castle and find something to share there.

Instead, she kicked at him. And then he kicked back. Soon they were in an epic battle. The children came closer again to cheer on the boy, whose name was apparently "Tough," or that's what it sounded like to her

He punched her in the face and she felt a tooth fall out. It was a baby tooth, but it hurt. It hadn't been ready to fall out.

She tried to punch him back, but he ducked the blow. He was clearly more used to fighting than she was. She'd never had to fight for anything in her life before.

In a moment, she realized he was mocking her, laughing at her with the crowd of children, which had grown. They all wanted to see her be hurt, to see her humbled.

He kicked at her leg, and she saw it bend below the knee in a way that it shouldn't. Then the pain struck, and she fell to the ground. She began weeping. She couldn't move. She was sure she was going to die from this pain.

The boy ran away then and left her there. All the children left. Abish dragged herself toward home, a few inches at a time. She howled and cried out for help, but no one seemed to hear her until she was within a few feet of her home. It was nearly dark then, and her father was in the house. He saw her and his face went still. Was her real father back again? Was she his princess again?

He ran toward her and picked her up in his arms. She wept at the touch of his hands on her broken leg. He called out for Timah and then laid Abish gently in the front room, sending her sisters to get her pillows and blankets. Her mother brought her hot tea and a wet cloth to wipe her face, which was covered with tears and snot.

In a little while, a doctor came. He pulled the bone straight again and splinted it, then wrapped it tightly and gave her instructions to remain in bed for three weeks at least, and then he would come again.

"Who was it who hurt you?" her father asked after the doctor had gone. He had sent all her sisters to bed, and Timah as well. He wanted to nurse his "princess" alone.

"One of the children. I tried to share with them," she insisted. "I really tried." She was afraid that he would punish her, even still.

"Of course you did. Give me a name or a description, Princess. I will make him or her wish they were never born," said her father.

She had a moment to decide if she wanted revenge on the boy who had hurt her. Her father could injure him far worse. And then what? The boy's family would be angry at her family, and it would never end. She'd only wanted someone to play with her, but that seemed impossible now.

She hadn't really tried to share, though. It had taken her until now to see her own fault in the matter. She'd been as much to blame as the boy. She shook her head. "I don't remember," she said.

"Abish, are you sure?" her father asked.

"There were too many of them, all around me. I was frightened, and I kept turning. I don't know who it was," she insisted.

Her father kissed her forehead and held her hand until she fell asleep. Twice in the night, when she woke up for a drink, he was there at her side.

"Princess," he said, "I love you. Never forget that. You are my life." And later she thought she heard him whisper in a dream, "They are not worthy of you, Princess. None of them."

3

Haman stopped taking Abish with him to his brick-building business when she was recovering from her injury, but he did not agree to take her again even when she was healed.

"It is too dangerous for you. I cannot always keep watch over you, and there are many things that grown men are injured on," her father said, as if he was suddenly conscious of all these fears.

No matter how Abish tried to beg and plead with him, Haman would not take her with him.

She tried once to follow him, but she was not far enough behind, and he caught her around a corner near the marketplace and dragged her back home.

He handed her to her mother at the door. "Keep her inside," he said.

Timah kept Abish inside by assigning her to her older sisters, who were annoyed to be given the task, but warmed up to it gradually as they saw how much it angered their spoiled younger sister. The more she struggled, the more they seemed to find it amusing.

For many months they did their work well and Abish had no chance to escape. But one day they had turned their back on her, sure that she had given up her foolish insistence to be with her father, and Abish made her own way to the brick building business. She had been with her father too many times to forget the many turns to take, and she was very good at remembering where things were.

She did not announce herself or go through the front door as a customer might. Instead, she went in the back door as the workers did. She waited until a group of them were all going inside and then pretended to be one of them. But she was too small and one of them saw her and yanked her aside by the hair.

"Who is this?" he said, and all the other workers laughed at her. Most of them knew Abish very well, and they also knew that she had been forbidden to come to the business.

The man who held her hair took her to her father.

Haman looked angry at her, but he did not tell her to go home—or take her himself. "Do you promise to do exactly what I tell you to do and to stand where I tell you to stand?" he asked.

"Yes, Father," she said eagerly.

"You must do it immediately. There are times when danger strikes and there are only seconds to react."

"I will do exactly as you say," she said. She was so tired of toys and of being seen as a child. She wanted to know what grown-ups did. She wanted to learn to do as they did.

She did everything her father asked her to do. She stood at his side. She said nothing when he needed silence to think or to talk to his men. She did not complain if she got dirty when she stepped into dirt. She became Haman's shadow. The men began to treat her as more than a child when they saw her. At first, they patted her head or gave her little treats. But as time passed, some would whisper to her before they turned to her father.

"What mood is he in today?" they would say.

And Abish would be truthful. "He's angry today." Or "he's tired." "Don't tell him that you're running late today." "He needs good news."

She had always loved her father, but this was the first time she saw him as a man instead of the man who loved her above all things. She learned what he was good at, pushing his men to perform and having the vision to build what other men dared not, and what he was not good at, keeping track of all the details and knowing the names and other truths about his men.

But Abish was good at these things too. She could see which men disliked each other, though her father assigned them to work together because of their skills. She worked in her own way to alleviate anger between them, to offer to take grievances to her father when the time was right, and to make sure he ate and rested well before the men had to present something difficult to him.

But she still felt that she was merely an appendage. She did nothing that was necessary. She understood the business, but she was sure that, if she tried to tell the men what to build, they would laugh at or ignore her. Or they would call her "Princess" derisively and then tell her precisely why everything she said to them was wrong.

She spent hours a day watching her father's men follow his plans step by step—or not. She learned what sloppy work was and what it cost. Her father sent men away if they did not work up to his standards, but he did not always see the problems as early as Abish did.

Once, she was standing at his side while he inspected the work of a building he had designed himself. It was for the king's cousin, and he had great hopes that it would be an entry into more work for the royal family. But the building listed to the side, and while her father stood there it began to sway.

There was only one moment to react. Her father pushed Abish out in front of him, covering her body with his own as she heard the terrible sound of a building of bricks crashing down around her. There was dust all over, and she could hardly breathe with her father's weight on top of her. She could hear the beat of her heart loudly in her ears.

At last her father stirred, and she realized that he was still alive.

"Father?" she said.

"Princess?" he asked.

"I'm here. I'm fine." She was bruised and frightened, but she was alive.

In a few minutes, his men came and began to unbury them.

Her father cursed at them when they helped him to his feet at last.

"You should go home now," he told Abish. He looked at one of his men and gestured to her. "You—take my daughter home where she will be safe."

Abish was tempted to argue with him, but she decided that now was not the right time. She would have other chances to convince her father to take her back with him, and she was truly shaken.

Later that week, Abish learned that all the men involved in this disastrous project were sent away. She watched as their families packed up their things and moved to another city, where their reputations were not ruined. She hoped they had learned something and would not do the same thing there.

"Please, can I come back with you?" Abish asked Haman when it was all over.

"No. It isn't safe." He looked away and Abish could see that he was still afraid.

"But I did what you said. I moved when you said to move," Abish said. "As long as you are with me, I will be safe."

"You are safe at home," said her father, who had begun to tremble.

Abish felt for her father, but she was not ready to simply stay at home. "What if there is an earthquake? What if I walk by another building that is ready to fall? There is no real safety anywhere. But I feel safest of all when I am with you, Father." This was the truth.

Her father looked her in the eyes. "Are you sure?" he asked.

She met his gaze with certainty. "Father, I trust you above all else. Please, let me go with you tomorrow."

So her father did. And after that, for reasons she did not understand, he seemed to trust her more. He let her stand further away from him and sometimes he even sent her to bring messages to his men. Abish had a chance to be seen as more than her father's princess, and she liked it.

Until she saw the light-skinned men who were enslaved, chained to each other and putting straw and mud together before it was put into molds. She had never seen this part of the business before. Her father had never taken her here when she was younger. She had assumed that the men who did this work were the same as any of the other workers her father hired.

"Who are they?" she asked one of her father's men.

He spat on the ground. "Nephites," he said.

31

Abish knew who the Nephites were. They were the enemy of her own people. They had descended from the treacherous brother Nephi, who had stolen so much from her ancestors Laman and Lemuel when the family had come to the Promised Land from Israel so many years ago.

"Why are they wearing chains? What have they done against us?"

"They don't need to do anything against us. They are slaves. They came into our land, and their very presence here is not allowed. Any who stray here become ours to work as we wish. We will not allow spies."

"But what if they did not know where they were going? They could have been lost." She did not believe any of these men were spies. Some of them looked very young, hardly older than she was.

"It does not matter. They are slaves now," said her father's man.

"But will they ever be set free?" she asked.

"Of course," said her father's man with a strange tone that made her fear him in a way she never had before. She had thought of him as a friend.

"When?" Abish asked. If they worked five years or ten, surely they could go home to their own families. She could not imagine that Nephite families loved their children as her mother and father loved theirs, but they could not be all bad.

"When they die," said her father's man, and spat again.

Abish asked her father about the slaves later. "Shouldn't they be allowed to go home someday?" she asked.

"Would you say that about our cattle?" her father asked in turn. "Our sheep and goats should be allowed to go free after they have given us milk for a time?"

"No, but—" Abish tried to say.

"It is the same with Nephites. They are animals. We own them if they come onto our land. If we let them go, they will only go back to their evil ways. This is our chance to civilize them. By hard work, they will learn important lessons."

Abish did not understand, but she did not want to go back to her father's business after that. She was too disturbed at the thought of where all her toys and jewels, her castle, her home, and all her precious clothing came from. The work of those men, slaves, Nephites.

She could not think of the Nephites as animals. They were men, as her father and his own workers were. Whatever their ancestors had done, they were not to blame. It seemed terrible to her that the foundations of so many buildings were built on the backs of these men, who would die in slavery, but any time she voiced this opinion out loud she was shouted down. By her mother, her sisters, and anyone Lamanite.

Whatever she chose to do with her future, Abish told herself that she would find a way to help the Nephite slaves in the city. She could talk to the king or bring them food or somehow open the eyes of others to their plight. She was not meant to be a brick builder. She had greater things in store for her life.

4

Everything changed when Tamar announced her betrothal to Laman, a handsome, tall, and well-spoken man from a wealthy family.

He had started courting Tamar when she was very young, only sixteen years old, but Haman had told him that he could not marry her until she was twenty-two.

Other men thought this was ridiculous and told Haman that he was ruining his daughter's chances for happiness. They said that Laman would give up and find another young woman he could marry much sooner. A man's attention could not be held for so long without any reward.

"Let him find someone else, then," Haman said many times over. "My daughter deserves a man who will not leave her at the first chance."

And so Laman waited. For six long years.

Abish had not thought he would last. She had not wanted Tamar to marry in any case, for then her sister would be gone, and the family would never be the same again. All of her sisters were so much older than Abish was. She did not want to be the only one left home alone.

Tamar herself had begged her father to allow her to marry Laman when she was twenty years old. By then he had already waited four years then to prove himself faithful, but Haman was immovable.

"We agreed that he would wait until you are twenty-two," he said.

"But Father, I am a grown woman now. My friends are all married already. They have children, many of them."

"Yes, they do," Haman said.

"Father, tell me why. Why must Laman do what no man has done in order to earn me?"

Haman told the story of his own mother's marriage, and the years it had taken his father to win her hand. She had been dubious that he was steady enough for her because he had been a wastrel in his youth.

"But that is different," Tamar insisted. "Laman has done nothing wrong. He has always been a good man. Why should he suffer for your father's sins?"

"Because my father loved my mother until her last breath, and I want to see you find a man who will do the same," Haman said.

"He loves me. He will love me forever, Father. He promised me that," said Tamar.

But Haman insisted that Tamar and Laman wait. And since he was the father they obeyed him.

Though there had been that time, when Tamar had just turned twenty-one, that Abish had caught her packing her things in a bag in the middle of the night.

Abish had been awake because she was ill, and had to hurry to the privy outside. When she came back in, feeling better, she noticed Tamar looking through the stores in the kitchen. "What are you doing?" she asked. She'd assumed that Tamar was ill too and was trying to find something to settle her stomach. "Can I have some tea?"

Tamar turned around, her eyes wide. "Abish, you must be quiet," she said. She put her arms around her sister from behind. "Go back to sleep and say nothing about seeing me tonight, please. If Father asks you in the morning, you can tell him then. But after I'm gone."

"Gone where?" Abish said.

"To Laman. He and I are running away together tomorrow to be married without Father's permission. We will have to live in another city, but it will be worth it."

"Another city?" Abish said. "But when will we see you? What about celebration days?"

"Father will relent in a little while," said Tamar, but she didn't sound very certain. "And then we will come back, and everything will be as it should have been from the beginning. Father has no right to tell us when to be married—not when I am already grown."

Abish considered this for a while. "Father will be very angry," she said. "And he is very proud."

"He is being completely unreasonable. Laman has already shown how much he loves me. There is no reason for us to wait another year."

Abish felt sick again. She put her hands to her stomach, but there was nothing left there. She realized she felt sick for Tamar now. "I will miss you very much," she said. She knew that Tamar had resented her for a long time after she was born, but still, she loved her sister. She did not want to say goodbye to her forever, but that seemed to be what Tamar was choosing.

What about Mother? And the other sisters? What about all of Tamar's friends who would never see her again?

"You are my least favorite sister," Tamar said.

"I know," Abish said tearfully.

"I won't miss you at all." Tamar's face twisted, like she was ready to cry.

"I know," Abish said again.

"Now, go back to bed and be quiet." Tamar pushed Abish back to her own room.

But in the morning Tamar was still there, and Abish never told her father that she had almost run away.

The plan now was for Tamar and Laman to live nearby. Laman worked as a carpenter and already had a home ready for them. Haman had insisted on giving a bride price to Laman, though he said it was unnecessary.

Both men were proud, Abish thought. She did not know if she ever wanted to be married. She could not imagine loving any man more than she loved her father, and she couldn't imagine a man treating her as well as her father did.

There were women who stayed with their parents all their lives, who cared for them until they died and then inherited their homes. Why shouldn't Abish wish for that? Her other sisters could all leave home, and Abish would stay.

Abish had to pick out a dress to wear to the wedding that would not "outshine Tamar," as her mother warned her. Their father gave Tamar a lavish silver and turquoise headpiece to wear on her wedding day. She cried over it and then kissed her father and told him that she loved him.

Her jealousy for Tamar lasted only one day, however. Two days after the wedding Abish saw her sister at the marketplace. Although Tamar's face was covered with a scarf, Abish could see the bruises on her arms. When Timah saw them she pulled Tamar to the side and tried to speak to her, but Tamar tightened her lips and looked away as if she did not know who her mother was.

A week later Abish heard that her father had gone to her sister's house and had beaten her husband to within an inch of his life.

In retaliation Laman began to spread rumors about Haman's business practices, and the two men became mortal enemies.

Though she had waited so long for her father's approval, Tamar did not come home even once after her marriage.

It seemed to Abish that marriage was not something to be wished for, so she was surprised when she discovered that her next oldest sister, Nesha, had given her heart to a man named Darius, who worked with her father.

He wasn't handsome or particularly tall, though he was thick with muscles. He spoke very little, and when he did speak, it was in a halting manner, as if he were ashamed of every word.

"He's just shy," said Nesha, if any of her sisters pointed out this flaw. "When we're alone, he has no problem speaking words of love to me."

Nesha was already twenty-one years old, and Abish expected her father to make the same rule for her that he had for Tamar, but he did not. He said that Nesha could marry whenever she chose, for he trusted Darius as he would his own son. The man had worked for him for ten years already, and he did what he was told and never left early.

Abish once overheard her parents talking about the upcoming wedding when they thought everyone else was in bed.

"He's not the smartest man I've ever known, but he'll never turn against me," Haman said.

"I trust that's true, but will he be able to support Nesha and any children they have together?" asked Timah.

"Shirking is not one of his weaknesses," Haman said.

"Is he the man you would give over the business to?" asked Timah.

Abish tensed at this. She had not thought of this as a possibility. Was it already time for her father to give over his business? Most men did that only when they were aging and could no longer work. They usually died shortly thereafter. She did not want her father to die. What would her life be if he was gone?

"I don't think so, but that doesn't mean he's not a good man. He will make Nesha very happy," Haman said.

There was a long pause. Then Timah said, "You don't think that Nesha deserves better?"

"She is in love with him. I see no reason to stand in her way."

They were both thinking of Tamar, Abish was sure. But neither of them spoke her name aloud. It was almost as if her oldest sister had been erased from the family. No one told stories about when Tamar was younger, even if the stories were mostly about someone else. It was too painful to talk about her when she had turned her back on them all.

"I wish there were some way to know everything about a man," Timah said.

"That is impossible. And even if we could know everything about him now, we would not know how he might change in the future."

"You can't marry a man and depend on him to change."

"I changed," Haman said.

"Yes." Timah's voice trembled with emotion. "You did indeed."

Were they both hoping that Laman would also change? Abish had heard that Tamar was expecting her first child. Of course, the midwife proclaimed loudly that she knew that it was a boy from the way that it protruded so far out, but until the child was born, no one would know for sure.

What would Laman do if his first child was a daughter? Or if he had seven daughters?

Abish shivered at the thought.

"We cannot get the perfect man for all our daughters," Haman went on.

"No? Is that because there is no perfect man or because there are not enough of them for seven girls?" Timah sounded bitter now.

"I haven't met one yet, in any case," Haman said. "If they are in love, what can we do? They will insist and refuse to see the truth if they do not wish to. We must allow our daughters to live their own lives once they are women."

That was what Tamar had asked for, and had not been granted. Would her life have been any different if Laman had not been forced to wait for her? They would never know now.

The next week, Nesha dressed in her perfect scarlet wedding gown, her hair curled and piled high above her head, jewels adorning her ears. She smiled so widely that Abish thought she might pull a muscle, but she didn't. She beamed radiantly at her husband as they held hands together over the fire, and then she kissed him in front of everyone without even blushing as they were declared husband and wife.

They danced, leading all the guests who had come, clapping their hands and singing along with the best musicians in the city. They ate and drank until long after dark. Then they were escorted to their own beds and left alone as the party went on without them for many hours.

Abish sat next to her father as the giant wedding bonfire died down. She was tired but not yet ready for bed. She wanted to hold onto this special moment in her family that seemed to promise so much. In the morning, who knew what would happen and what reality would have to be faced?

"Darius is enough for Nesha, but I will not have such a man marry you, Princess," her father whispered in her ear.

It had been a long time since her father had called her that. Did he still think of her that way? She craned her head back to look at her father. "What do you mean?"

"You must have the best man in the city to wed. You deserve all that is right and good in the world."

Abish had never told her father that she did not intend to marry. "Who do you think is the best man in the city?" she asked in a teasing tone. "The prince? The king himself?"

Her father had started building for the king's stables, and she thought he had met the man himself, since the king loved his horses and rode them as often as he wanted regardless of how it affected his royal regalia.

Haman shook his head. "No, not the king. I know him too well. He has been married twice already, and I would not want him for my favorite daughter. As for the prince, well, he seems uninterested in a bride. He is too busy spending his father's money. I hope that someday he will mature into the crown, but I have no proof it will happen soon enough for you." He kissed her on the nose.

"Then who?" Abish said. She wanted to prepare herself if she had to, to tell her father she did not wish to marry.

But he only said, "I don't know. I'm waiting for the right man. Surely I'll meet him at some point. Every time a man comes to commission a building, or to work with me, I evaluate him for you Abish. And they all fall short."

"And why is that?" she asked, curious now.

"One man is too short, another too tall. This man is fat. That one farts too much. This one is known to be mean to his cattle. That one reads all day long. This one eats messily. That one has put his sisters away to avoid paying a bride price for them." He shook his head. "There will be a man for you, Abish. But I must look carefully for him. We have only a few years still."

5

When Tamar gave birth to a boy, the news came to Haman and Timah. Haman refused to step into "that man's home," but Abish went with her mother to visit her sister. They brought with them a gift for the child, a new warm blanket for the coming winter, and a gift for the mother, a nut cake that Timah had made herself with a jewel in the center for Tamar to keep—or sell, if she wished.

Haman sent this message with his wife: "Tell Tamar that if she wishes to leave her husband she and her son may come home, and we will welcome them with open arms."

Abish was uncomfortable at the thought of trying to say this to Tamar, and Timah seemed equally so, for she never said a word of it on their visit. She only said, "your father wanted me to tell you that he loves you and thinks of you often."

For the first time in her life, Abish had begun to see her father's flaws. Oh, she'd always known that he had a quick temper. She'd known that he treated her differently than he treated her sisters, though she thought this was because she deserved it.

Now she saw her father as a man who was too proud to do all he could to help his daughter, even if he loved her. She saw, too, that her father's special love for his youngest daughter was unfair. If he loved Tamar as much, he would do more for her. Or would he?

It occurred to Abish to wonder if there were something she could do to lose her father's love. What if she had threatened to run away and marry a man her father did not like?

Abish kissed her sister's cheek gently because there were fading bruises there. When had her husband last beaten her? Had he not even feared hurting his own child? "How are you?" she asked.

"I am very well," Tamar assured her. "We are calling him Laman, after his father."

"That is a good name," Abish said. She hoped it would help protect her sister and the child if the father thought of him as his namesake.

"Isn't he beautiful?" said Tamar, opening the blankets around his face so that he could be seen.

The babe was handsome and looked very much like his father. His tiny fist reached for Tamar's and grasped it.

"You see? He knows me. He knows that I am his mother and that I love him," said Tamar, pinching the baby's cheeks.

"May I hold him?" Abish asked. As the youngest of seven daughters she'd had little chance to hold a baby before. She might have asked neighbors, but she'd never been much interested in smaller children.

Tamar looked at Timah.

"I'm sure your sister can hold a baby. She's not completely useless you know," Timah said.

Abish was stung with this, because her mother seemed to think her useless in many ways. But Tamar lifted little Laman up to her.

The smell of him was uniquely attractive. He weighed so little but wiggled so much.

"Hold his head," Tamar coaxed Abish. "He can't hold it up himself yet. And make sure you don't strangle him."

Abish tried to follow Tamar's rules, but it all seemed very complicated. She handed young Laman back quickly to Tamar, who passed him to her mother.

Timah had no difficult holding the baby boy in her arms. It looked like she had never stopped holding a child, she was so adept at it. She bounced back and forth to settle his cries and then danced and sang with him in a voice so sweet that Abish wondered if she'd heard the same songs herself when she was a baby. She did not remember them now.

Soon Laman was asleep, and Timah put him into his cradle. It looked very well made.

"His father made that for him," said Tamar proudly. "He dotes on his son."

It was good that Tamar had a boy first, thought Abish.

"Are you taking care of yourself?" Timah asked her daughter, giving her her full attention now.

"I'm fine, Mama," said Tamar.

"Have you been up walking since the birth?" Timah asked.

"No, I don't want to," said Tamar.

"You must get up. You have to get your legs warm again. It is the most important part of your recovery. My midwife told me every time I had a child to get up again as soon as I could."

"Well, my midwife said no such thing," Tamar argued.

But Timah pushed Tamar to her feet and took her on a brief walk around the room before allowing her to lie back again.

"And what about food and drink? Are you eating enough? It takes a lot of food for a woman to make milk for a son."

"I'm fine, Mama," Tamar said again.

"Eat some cake," Timah said, and she watched as Tamar chewed at the cake. Something seemed wrong with her jaw. She didn't chew easily. Had her husband hit her there so badly that it still hurt? Were her teeth loose?

Tamar saw the jewel inside the cake as she tried to take a second piece. "Mama!" she said with a smile.

"Your father sent that," Timah said, though that was a blatant falsehood.

"Oh," said Tamar after a moment. "I can't keep it. You'll have to take it back to him with you. Laman would see it as a statement that he could not support us on his own."

"Keep it," Timah said. "You may need it in the future."

"But—" Tamar protested.

"Hide it in some of the baby's dirty things. Laman will never poke around in those. But you must have some security for yourself and your son. I know that Laman is very sweet right now, but what about in two months? Or two years?"

Tamar took a long breath, and her face fell. "All right, Mama," she said softly, and tucked the jewel away.

Abish thought again of her vow never to marry. She would never have children then. She would never feel the way that Tamar felt as she looked at her son. Was that a good thing or a bad one?

"I will come and see you again next week. You should be walking easily by then," Timah said, shaking a finger at her daughter. "Remember that as long as the babe is sleeping, you should sleep too. And tell Laman that he must sleep separately for at least six weeks."

Tamar spluttered at this. "Six weeks?" she said, astonished.

"Yes, six weeks. If your midwife did not tell you that, she was a fool. A woman needs time to herself, to heal. Giving birth is hard work, and there are wounds that your husband may not see but which are still there. Would he demand a man go back to the battlefield if he was still bleeding?" she asked.

Tamar blushed at this and looked down to see if there were spots of blood on the bed, but there were none. "Mama, I can't ask my husband to sleep in a different room for six weeks."

"Then have him sleep on the floor. Then he can get up to fetch the baby for you in the night."

"Mama, you know he will not do that. And besides, you said that it was good for me to get up and walk."

"In the daytime, yes," Timah said. "And without the weight of the babe in your arms."

But Tamar shook her head and bit down on her lower lip.

Abish knew that what she was not saying was that, if she asked her husband for this, she would get another beating, and that would not be good for her or her son, either.

"That man should be kicked between his legs," Timah muttered as they walked back to their own home. "And if he has no more children, all the better for Tamar. Some men think they own their wives and children like they own their cattle. It shouldn't be that way."

Abish thought of her father's threat to kill her mother if she had a seventh daughter. What had made him change so dramatically? He had never told her.

At home the next day Haman announced that Zara, his third daughter, was to be married the next month.

"What is this? I've not heard a word about it!" Timah declared. She turned to her daughter, who was smiling broadly as if she'd played a trick on her mother.

Zara was only nineteen years old, which was not so young that anyone would say a word against the marriage, but was younger than either Tamar or Nesha had been. But age had not saved Tamar, so perhaps their father had given that up.

"I introduced her to Jakob, my right-hand man," Haman said. "I did not want to trouble you, but I hoped they would take to each other, and they have." He seemed very pleased with himself.

"Jakob? The one with the blonde hair?" asked Timah.

"The very one. He's handsome enough for our daughter, isn't he?" Haman said.

Abish remembered Jakob from her early years in her father's business. He'd been much more junior then, just one of the men who helped to coordinate the eastern side of the city's building, but he'd been smart and eager to work. Was he the man her father would give his business to, since he had no sons of his own? Abish struggled with a sense of jealousy despite the fact that she had not been to her father's business in more than a year.

"Why didn't you invite him to meet all of us before the betrothal was official?" Timah was clearly hurt that this had happened without her knowledge.

"I wanted to surprise you," said Haman, who now seemed to be regretting it. "I thought you would be pleased to see another daughter happily married."

Another daughter? Was he counting Tamar in that? Abish wished her father had at least gone to see his grandson.

"Is there a reason for the hurry?" asked Timah.

"No reason but Zara's eagerness. All of her friends are already being married off. She didn't want to be left behind," Haman said.

Timah forgave her husband soon enough and invited Jakob for dinner to meet the whole family. He was a steady man, though he seemed more interested in the business than in marriage. He talked more to Haman about his plans than he did to Zara. But she was thrilled with him, keeping her arm in his throughout the night, and bragging to her younger sisters that she had the best man of them all.

It wasn't until weeks later, when Abish went to bring her father his lunch, that she began to understand his eagerness to marry Zara to Jakob. He was alone in his own office with none of his men around, but his face showed clear lines of pain, and he limped badly whenever he tried to move.

"Father, what is wrong?" Abish asked.

He waved a hand. "It's nothing, Princess. I'm a little tired, that's all." And after that, he tried to make sure that he showed no sign of the pain. His mouth twisted into a smile, and he forced his leg to take his full weight.

Abish was not convinced. She watched her father more carefully the rest of the week, and she could see moments when he thought no one was looking that he rubbed his leg and showed pain on his face. Timah knew nothing about it; that was clear. But when Jakob was nearby, Abish could see that her father let his assistant help him.

"I know you are in pain, Father," Abish said to him one night when Timah had already gone to bed.

"It's not so bad," Haman said. He wasn't trying to pretend it did not exist anymore. He reached for a chair and settled himself onto it gently, moving his leg out straight so he could rub it. "I'm lucky to be able to move at all at my age." He tried to smile at this.

Abish had never thought of her father as old before. Yet now she calculated his age and realized he must be nearly fifty. Few men lived much past that age. He had seven daughters and had lived a good life. Yet she was not ready to say goodbye.

Abish moved closer to her father and tried to rub his leg for him. He closed his eyes and leaned back, eager for her soothing touch. He made a low moaning sound as she found the right spot.

"Jakob has been doing much of my business when my leg aches. He makes sure that no one sees me as infirm. The wrong rumors could ruin the business, and Jakob doesn't want that anymore than I do."

"And is that why you wanted Zara to marry him?" Abish said. Was her sister a reward for loyalty? Did Zara understand anything that was going on here?

"I would never have forced her if she did not like the man," Haman said, opening his eyes at staring at Abish. He was defensive now and Abish realized that he did not use the word "love."

"Does she know about your leg?" Abish asked.

Haman shook his head briefly. "But I told her that I plan to give the business to Jakob in the next year. So she will be a wealthy woman."

Far wealthier than either of the other two sisters who had been married. Was it fair? Abish didn't know.

"And what about Mama and the rest of us?" Abish asked. Was her father going to be in a hurry to marry them all off?

"I have offered Jakob a partnership," he explained easily, as if it was something rehearsed. "He will continue to work, and I will consult, so I will continue to earn part of the company's income yearly until I die. After that, your mother will inherit my stake and will take ten percent."

Abish was good enough at math to know that was not nearly what her mother lived on now. Would they be able to stay in the same house? There would be many economies to make. And all that depended on Jakob following a commitment he had made to a man who was no longer alive to enforce the deal.

"I don't want you to die," she said softly. She had been so busy following the math that she had not let herself feel the fear of her father's mortality.

"And I don't want to die either. But it will come. Hopefully not for some years yet. But I am an old man now." He rubbed at his gray hairs. He had always been so strong, capable of anything. And now?

Abish's plan for her life had included her father continuing to live for a long time. She had wanted to help him in his late years, but she had not thought they would come so soon.

"My hope is that I will be able to marry the others off as soon as they find someone they love," Haman continued. "And as for you, we will have to wait for your prince." He smiled gently. "Or for someone close enough to him for you to consent to."

Her father had never suggested that she might need to marry for reasons other than love. Now Abish began to see more clearly that this might no longer be possible.

"When will you tell Mother?" Abish asked.

"In time," Haman said. This thought seemed to pain him more than his leg, for he had stopped rubbing the physically injured part of himself and had begun to rub his head instead.

6

The wedding for Zara and Jakob was the most elaborate Abish had ever seen. There were three days of feasting, the day before the wedding, the day of the wedding, and the day after the wedding. Zara's dress was made by a seamstress who had made the queen's own wedding gown, and the fabric was imported from the far north. It was a shimmering lavender so light it looked white in some lights, and Zara looked far more the princess than Abish ever had.

She wore a headdress that looked like nothing so much as a princess's crown and was decorated in diamonds of all different colors: ice blue and pink and purple, green and yellow. She was carried to the center square on the back of a llama and walked in on heeled shoes that made her several inches taller. Her cheeks had been reddened with dye, and her hair had lengths added to it so she could pile it high on her head and still have enough left to fall over her shoulders.

Jakob looked modest in comparison, though he wore a jeweled headband and matching jewels on his shoes and arms. Abish had heard the arguments between him and her father about how much money to spend on the wedding. Jakob wanted to make sure that his wife was seen as the most beautiful woman in the city and that their wedding reminded every man who might be considering building that Jakob was a man of reputation and honor.

"Jewels do not make a man of reputation and honor," Haman argued in return.

"Not when you married, but now the world has changed," Jakob insisted.

And so in the end, every part of the wedding was elaborate, expensive, and shown to the world.

Timah and Haman were transported to the wedding in a chariot harnessed to perfectly white goats. Timah wore the same lavender as her daughter did, but without a headdress. Instead, her ears and neck were adorned in emeralds.

Haman also wore jewels on his shoes, though Abish knew that her father had been resting for two days so that his leg could get through all of the public events of Zara's wedding. He wanted to stand without shaking throughout the whole ceremony, and to be able to greet the wedding guests, as well.

He was only successful in the first of these hopes, for after only a few minutes of greeting guests, his bad leg simply collapsed, dropping him to the ground and soiling his fine wedding clothes. He tried to get to his feet and pretend it had been a joke, but in another few minutes he was down on one knee again.

"My new father has had a difficult day," Jakob said and called for a chair to be brought so that Haman could continue with Timah and the newlywed couple. But Haman insisted on standing each time a new person came to shake his hand. He would only sit for a few minutes before dragging himself up, hopping around on one leg because the bad one would hold no weight.

Abish could see the sweat dripping down his face as he tried to pretend he was still young. Her heart ached at her father's pride.

After the first day of feasting, Abish had an idea to help Haman. Since the entire city had been invited to the wedding—including even the poorest and lowliest citizens, who had come both for the free food and wine as well as the spectacle of the event—Abish began to circulate among the guests to find a healer who might help her father. She finally found one who claimed that he had a potion that could cure any weakness in any muscle—for a price.

"My father can pay well for your services," Abish insisted as she pulled him towards her father.

She introduced the two of them, but her father was too embarrassed to speak to the man in public, so they made arrangements for him to come to the house the day after the wedding festivities.

Abish stayed at her father's side all day and all night. He refused to hire a vehicle to carry him home, but he also refused to hang on his wife and daughter to walk slowly. He said that he would sleep where he was, and they could all say that he was too drunk to move.

Abish wept and refused to go home alone, so she stayed with her father and slept next to him in the street. She heard him crying out in pain all night long, and in the morning her mother brought the healer to them. The man did not bother to examine the leg. He simply gave a potion to Haman and told him the price of it.

Haman drank the potion down with a clear look of disgust and then handed the bottle back to the healer, along with the coin he had asked for.

But the potion did nothing to help him that day. His leg still did not allow him to walk unaided, but he seemed a little more tractable. He allowed Abish to help him home, and he sang and called out to others with a wave, as if he were drunk. As soon as he arrived at home, he sank to the floor and asked Abish to bring him a pillow and blanket so he could sleep. He did not wake until the next evening, and Abish checked him many times to make sure that he was still breathing.

The next day, when he woke at last, all the pain in his leg had returned twice over. And after that, Haman did not go to the business. He said that he would go the next day, but each morning when he tried to get to his feet again, he collapsed.

Abish searched far and wide in the city to find other healers who promised to help, but her father grew angrier and more resistant each time they arrived with their remedies. After the first three, he refused to drink any of their potions and would not hold still for examinations or attempts to rub at the muscles in the leg.

"Leave an old man alone!" he shouted.

He was an old man indeed now. His speech seemed slurred, and his whole left side did not move properly, not just his leg. Abish was not sure if this was the result of the potion he had taken, something else that had happened, or simply the progress of whatever it was that had damaged his leg in the first place.

Worst of all, her father did not call her "Princess." Instead, he called her "Girl" or "Daughter" or "Child," but always with a twist to his face, anger in his every word. He treated her as a slave more than a beloved daughter, and though she loved her father dearly and told herself that he did not understand what he was doing to her, it was difficult sometimes to help him—or even to be near him.

Jakob came a few times after the wedding to discuss the business he had now taken control of entirely. When this happened, Haman commanded everyone to leave the room so that they could have privacy.

Abish wanted to obey her father's wishes, but she was afraid of what Jakob might be doing without her father's supervision. She wanted to go into the business herself and look around, ask the friends she still had there what had happened now that Jakob was in charge, but she dared not do it when that would mean leaving her father behind.

After many days and nights of caring for her father despite his rages and threats, Abish found him tearful and penitent one night, long after her mother was in bed. She sat beside him and touched his arm soothingly and he leaned toward her and blew her a kiss.

"My princess," he said again.

"My father," she said, weeping that the man she had loved for so long had come back to her. She did not know how long it would last, but she would enjoy the moment her father seemed to have set aside his pain and found his love for her again.

"I have been so terrible to you," Haman said. "You must forgive me."

"Of course I forgive you, Father," Abish said. She would always forgive him.

He nodded. "You have always been good to me, far better than I have deserved." He kissed her hair and patted her head as if she were still a little girl. She was as tall as her oldest sisters now, and though she would never be as tall as her father while standing, he did not stand now, and she towered over the body lying on the bed.

"Oh, Father, don't say that. You know that you have treated me as a princess. I have been blessed to have you as my father."

Haman closed his eyes for so long that Abish thought he must have fallen back asleep. She tried to ease away from him so he could rest fully flat on the floor, but he pulled her back. His grasp was weak, but she did not resist it.

"What is it, Father?" she asked.

"You say I have been good to you, but that has only been true since my vision."

"Vision?" What vision did he have? Was this since he'd injured his leg? Since the wedding? When?

"At your birth. It was what protected you from my wrath. I raised my hand to strike you dead as an infant, and then I was struck down by an unseen force. I fell into the other world, and what I saw there frightened me into changing who I was."

"What did you see there?" Abish asked. This must be what her father had always held back from her, since she had first learned that he had threatened to kill her if she was born a girl, the seventh girl his wife had given him.

"I saw the One True God and His Son. I saw my ancestors. And I saw myself as I might have become if I had continued on the path that I was on." His words were barely more than a whisper, as if his strength were leaving him.

Abish wanted to tell her father to save his strength, but she also wanted to know more of this secret he had kept from her for so long. "What of the other gods?" she asked.

All her life she had been taught about many gods and how to worship each of them in their own particular way. The gifts to the god of the trees, the murmured prayers to the sun god, the way to raise a hand to the wind god, and on and on. She had always observed all of the rules, but she knew that her father had not. Some might say that his illness had come upon him because of his lack of devotion, but she did not believe this was so. Though she had gone through the motions her whole life, she had felt nothing for any of the gods. There was only emptiness there.

"Abish, there are no other gods. You must know this before I die, and you must promise to keep it to yourself. You must swear to me that you will tell no one." His grip on her upper arm was as tight as it had ever been, and for a moment Abish hoped that he was coming back to his strength.

"Of course, Father," she said. But she wanted to know more. Who was the One True God? What was He like? Who was His son? Did they rule over the other gods?

She stared at her father, holding her burning questions inside, for he looked weaker than ever. His head sagged back. Spittle pooled in the side of his mouth, and his eyes stared straight above.

"Father?" she asked softly.

He jerked upright again, and looked at her. "You know that the Nephites worship the one God?" he whispered.

"Yes," Abish said.

"It was their God I saw in my vision. Their God of all, and the son who is to come to earth as a sacrifice for sin. The one born of a virgin."

Abish's eyes widened. She did not know even this much about the Nephite god. She did not know how her father had learned so much. It was blasphemy for him to know any of this, let alone to pass it along to her.

Yet she listened because she had never felt such a warmth, such a sense of completeness as he spoke. It was nothing like the cold emptiness she felt when speaking of the Lamanite gods.

Haman shook himself and then continued, his voice as a thread. "I told you, I saw myself as I would have been, if I had not changed. I saw that I had become a well of darkness and that there was no one who wished to be near me. My ancestors turned away from me and refused to hear my calls for them. I was utterly alone. It was the worst thing I could imagine." He let out a long, shuddering breath, clearly in pain but fighting to stay alive and keep his words clear for her.

"Father?" Abish said. She could not bear that he seemed so close to death. She wanted to talk to him about all the things he had done that made her love him—not this dream that she could never speak of to anyone lest she endanger herself.

Haman coughed weakly, trembling, though his voice sounded strong again. "Abish, listen to me. I know that it is dangerous to worship the Nephite god. I don't ask you to do it openly. But you must know in your heart that He is the only God. There are no other gods, only imaginations we have created in our heads because we wanted something but could not follow the Nephites. Do you understand? It is because of our fathers' traditions, because of their pride. We could not admit the truth." He was holding very tightly to her hand now, but she dared not complain.

"Yes, Father," Abish said. Tears were welling up in her eyes. She could feel that this was her father's final message to her. She could not turn away from it. She had to honor him in this moment, and that meant promising him anything he asked, no matter what the cost for her personally.

He went on in a moment, still holding her hand tightly, but as if he had forgotten that she was there, staring into the stars. "I saw you, Abish. Not as the infant you were then, but as the woman you have become now. And I saw that you had a special mission. You were sent here by God to help all of the Lamanites return to the true God. He loves us and wants us to return. All of us, even me. And he sent me that vision so that I would not kill you, and so that you could save me, as well."

Now Abish was stunned. She knew she was her father's princess, but she had never thought that meant anything other than being spoiled. He thought she had a mission to save her people? How? When he was dying, and she was only the daughter of a builder?

The Lamanites were many, many cities, and kingdoms beyond that. They spread out over the whole land where the Nephites did not live. How could she save so many thousands of them when she had never seen this One True God herself? She was not the real king's daughter. She was not even married. She had no children and was not sure that she ever would. She had only a portion of her father's business, and she wasn't even sure about now that Jakob had taken over.

But she did not tell her father any of this. She said only, "I will do anything I can, Father, if it will save you."

"Not this life," her father said, nodding at his old, infirm body. "I ask you to save my eternal life, my princess. My very soul. Abish, it depends on you. You must pray to the One True God yourself and hear what He says to you. Kneel down now and ask him to guide you." He let go of her hand at last and motioned vaguely down.

Abish did immediately as he indicated, though when she got to the floor she felt terribly uncomfortable. She had never prayed to any of the gods this way, and even when she had prayed she had never heard anything like an answer. "Now what?" she prompted, not sure that her father remembered that she was there with him.

He coughed again, and the sound made her heart ache. Her father was so far gone—a shadow of the strong man he had once been. And yet his mind was still strong, and so was his will.

"Just speak to Him as you would to any man," Haman urged softly. "Tell Him what is in your heart. Tell Him that you don't know what to do."

Abish hesitated. Was anyone listening? What should she say? But her father was asking her to grant his dying wish. She must say something.

Finally, she got out some halting words. "O God of the Nephites," she said, "My father tells me that you know me and that you have a great mission for me. But I feel . . .I am too young and too weak to save anyone. I don't understand what you would have me do." She looked at her father. What else could she say?

He simply nodded his weary head. "Yes," he said. "That will do."

After a moment, Abish said, "But now what?" Was that all? Could she stand again? Hold her father's hand again?

A wheeze from her father, who waved an ineffectual hand at her again. "Now you wait, my little princess. Kneeling. And listening. He will speak to you, Abish." More wheezing. "He knows who you are. He knows what you need . . . right now. He has been . . . watching you your whole life, and even before that."

Before that? What did her father mean?

"He has—prepared you for this, my little princess," he finished and began coughing again, the sound wet and terrifying.

But Abish remained on her knees as she had been instructed, trying to feel or hear something—anything—from this One True God.

Her father wheezed and coughed. And then he wheezed less.

Was he getting better? Was the One True God going to save his life, after all?

Abish's knees were sore and she had to rock back and forth to keep herself kneeling. She could feel the bruises rising and was afraid that soon she would break skin and begin to bleed. She was trying to listen, but she was not sure that she believed.

"Father?" she whispered after a long silence. Why was there no more coughing.

"*I'm here, Abish,*" she heard, but it took her a moment to realize it was not Haman's voice she heard, but a different Father, the One True God.

"You," she whispered.

"*I am here, Abish. I am with you. I have always been with you. I am your Father, and I have been waiting for you to come to me.*"

"But what am I to do? I'm not—I'm just a girl."

"*For now, Abish, you have only to pray to me and hear my voice when I speak in return. Can you do this?*"

"Y—yes," Abish stammered.

"*Then you will receive the blessings of my Holy Spirit to guide you, and the feelings of peace and calm and love in your heart.*"

With that, Abish felt as if she had been washed clean, and that all of her fears and worries about her father, her mother and sisters, her mortal life, were gone. She felt a warmth inside of her heart that she had never known before. She knew that this One True God loved her more deeply than she could comprehend and that nothing she did or did not do would ever separate them again.

"Thank you," she said.

But there was no answer this time. She felt that there was a connection still, but the voice had gone.

She looked back at her father. This time she saw that he was still, and when she bent to feel if he was still breathing, she knew that he was gone. There was no life left in him. Her father had died as she had been praying.

She had followed his last wish for her, but still she wept bitterly. She had wanted to say goodbye to him.

And then she thought about the other voice she had heard, the voice of love and promises. It was not her father's voice, but she felt sure that her father was not gone. The One True God had taken her father to him, and unlike the Lamanite gods, who fed the dead to the animals of the earth, she knew that the One True God offered eternal life. Her father was not truly dead, but alive again with the Nephite God who could not die.

"Father, I love you," she murmured. "Thank you for all you did for me."

There was no voice speaking to her now, but she felt sure that her father had embraced her in spirit, and she could let him go.

She fell asleep next to his body and did not wake until she heard her mother coming into the room hours later, and then she heard her mother's shriek when she realized that her husband had died.

Abish did not think she could have made it through that terrible day without the promise in her heart that she would see her father again in that other world—and the knowledge that the other father who loved her was at her side, helping her through every hard thing she had to do to prepare for the funeral and carrying her when she could no longer move herself.

7

The morning after the funeral Abish woke full of hope for the future. Her father had died, but the gift he had given her—telling her of his vision and teaching her to pray to the One True God—was so enormous that she could not imagine not feeling as complete as she did now. She only had to close her eyes to feel the One True God with her. Though she knew she could tell no one, not even her sisters, it didn't matter. The One True God seemed to hold her in His arms and fill her with love whenever she faltered.

"Let's sit down and talk about the future," Abish said to her mother after they had eaten a simple meal of the food that was left in the house. No one had gone out to the marketplace since her father had fallen ill, and there was nothing fresh left to eat, but Abish's sisters could be sent out to do that once she had had a chance to discuss things with her mother. They had to plan her father's funeral and think about how to make economies if they were to live on the allowance that her father arranged with Jakob to provide for them after his death.

"If you are going to tell me that I should marry again, I will not speak to you," Timah warned. "I loved your father with a depth and breadth that I cannot imagine feeling for another man. I had the chance to see him change from a boy to a man, and from a man to a saint. I don't imagine I will find that in any other Lamanite in all the lands."

"Mother, I'm not talking about marriage. I'm talking about the household funds. Have you spoken to Jakob? Do you know what he told Father?"

"Only that he would care for us," Timah said.

"But how many senines do you need?" Abish asked.

"I don't know. I never needed to count them before," Timah said.

Abish let out an impatient breath. She was certain that whatever Jakob had told her father, he would not give them unlimited funds.

She would have to count up the senines herself and go to Jakob to ask for a reasonable allowance.

Timah's mouth twisted. "Your sisters will not like to be told that they can no longer buy whatever dresses and baubles they wish for."

"Well, things will have to change. Father is—no longer here to provide for them." It seemed that Abish had not been the only princess in the home, even if it was her father's pet name for her. They would all have to begin to make economies. They would all have to learn the real value of a senine.

"But we must keep up appearances, surely," Timah said. "Your father would not want you to be seen as suddenly poverty-stricken. And you will all still need to attract husbands."

Besides Abish, three unmarried sisters remained at home: Lani, Gala, and Jenan. They ranged from fourteen to eighteen years of age. Lani might be old enough for marriage, and Gala might be old enough for an engagement, but Jenan was still far too young to have anything to do with men.

It felt strange for Abish to think of her sisters as added burdens to the household, but it had to be done. "Is there

66

any man in particular who has shown interest in Lani or Gala?" Abish asked.

A wave of the hand. "I think Belal asked for your father's permission to court Lani, but that was before Zara married. I don't know what arrangement they came to in the end, if any," Timah said. She seemed very tired and kept putting her head on the table. Abish did not think that she had eaten anything of the food she kept moving around her plate, but she did not know how to convince her mother to do so. One day without food would probably not harm her. But what about the day after that? Timah needed to learn to live without Haman.

"I'll ask Lani, then," Abish said. And Gala, as well. She did not want to push them out of the house, but things would be easier on the others, and on her mother, if there were fewer mouths to feed—or dresses to buy.

However, a wedding would be difficult to put on, considering their new budget. It was the bride's family's responsibility to put on the feast and to make the bride the envy of the city, but perhaps the groom could be persuaded to help? Or Jakob might wish to do it, for the sake of his wife's family and the business that had once belonged to Haman?

"We will manage, Mother," Abish said, putting her hands over her mother's. "You need not worry about us."

Timah let out a sound that was half-sigh, half-cry. "We will live, is what you mean. We will live, but will we want to live? I would rather be with your father, even if it is in death, than to try to live on without him."

Abish looked at her mother's drawn face and felt a deep fear settle into her. If her mother were to die, as well, would Jakob have any legal obligations to them at all? What would she and her sisters do? Would any of the older sisters take them in? Abish could not imagine asking Laman and Tamar to take them. Nesha and Darius would not be as bad, but they were expecting a child and trying to save money for the future.

"Mother, you cannot leave us," Abish said, gripping her hands more tightly and trying to put her face directly into her mother's. She met her mother's eyes and held them. "We need you here. Father must do without you for a little while longer."

Timah rocked back and forth, making a low sound of distress, almost like a trapped animal. "You don't understand. You can never understand."

"Mother." Abish spoke firmly. "I do understand. I loved Father. My life will never be the same without him. But we must go on. We have other obligations. You have seven daughters and we need you."

This did not seem to make her mother pay attention, so Abish tried something else. "Mother. Listen to me. Do you know that Father believed he would see you again?"

"Yes, I know that."

"I believe it, too. In another world, we will all be together." Abish didn't dare say anything directly about the One True God, but even this seemed dangerous.

"What difference does that make?" Timah asked.

"If you see Father again, what will you tell him? That you abandoned your daughters? Do you want to explain to him that you left us alone and impoverished when you could have chosen to stay? He had no choice, but you do. Do you want him to despise you for weakness?" Abish's whole body was tense. She hated having to say this to her own mother, but she had to anchor Timah to this life somehow, and if the only way to do that was to add to her guilt, she would do what she had to.

Timah bowed her head, her breaths coming like sobs. "You are cruel, Abish. I never knew you were so cruel." But she did not speak any more about dying, and when Abish reminded her that she must eat to remain strong, she did. Not much, but enough that Abish stopped bothering her.

It was something. It was one day, and Abish hoped it was the worst day.

But it was not the worst day.

One week after Haman's death, there was a knock at the door. Five men stood there, two of whom Abish recognized from her father's business.

"Hello, Gravam. Hello, Gewar. Welcome," she beckoned them inside, unsure why they had come.

Were they here to make a complaint about Jakob, now that he had taken over her father's role as head of the business? There was nothing Abish or her mother could do to help them now, but she would listen and try to offer them advice.

Gravam hung his head. "You will not welcome us when you read this." He handed Abish a scroll.

She unrolled it and felt her breath leave her chest. Surely this was not possible. Even Jakob could not be so cruel.

She did not move, did not shout, did not do anything for far too long.

And while she did not move, Gewar and the three men that Abish did not recognize moved past her to the other parts of the house. They began to move things and then to carry them out of the house.

The sound brought Lani and Gala downstairs as well as Timah. "What is happening?" they all asked.

Abish could not find the words to tell them, so Gravam simply handed them the scroll.

"This is impossible," Timah said. Her voice was unsteady, her face pale and terrified.

Abish stared at her mother, afraid she would physically collapse right there. She could not stop the men if she had to think about her mother's life. Jakob had not kept his promise to their father about their mother's allowance, but they still needed her. They all needed her to keep them together as a family, even if Abish had no idea now where they would live.

"You are to be out of the house within a day's time," Gravam said coldly. It was only what the scroll said. There was no compassion in his voice, though Abish had once thought of him as a friend. What had Jakob threatened him with to change him so?

"I must go to see Jakob. Surely this is a misunderstanding," Timah said. For the first time since Haman's death she seemed herself again. There was strength in her tone, certainty in her words.

Abish didn't know if she should go with her mother to protect her from whatever Jakob would say to her, or if she should stay at home to minimize the destruction done here. They would need to gather as much as they could by the next morning. Clothing, anything they could sell for money, a little food. She should be making a list.

She was surprised that she was no longer thinking about how terrible it was that Jakob had done this. Instead, she was trying to figure out how they would survive. They would need to move in with Nesha and Darius. She should send one of her sisters to speak to them, to make sure they would be ready.

"Lani," Abish said. "You must—" she started to say.

"Don't you tell me what to do. You are my younger sister, not my mother. I'm going to Belal to tell him that we must marry now—today," said Lani, her face red, but her head held high.

"Mother must give you permission," Abish said. "Now that Father is . . ." she could not bring herself to say the words quite yet.

Timah did not seem capable of processing anything that Lani said. "Jakob," she said aloud as she gathered her shawl. "I must go to see Jakob."

"Mother! Tell Lani that she must stay with us. She cannot marry in one day's time." It would look terrible and mark her as desperate. The whole city would be filled with rumors and that would not help any of the rest of them. They would all need to marry in time. Even Abish herself, she realized.

"I will do as I please," Lani insisted.

Abish saw now that Lani had already packed a bag for herself. Had she known that Jakob would do this? Had Zara warned her? Or had she simply made this decision once she'd larned that Father was dead?

"But what does Belal expect from your family?" Abish asked. The bride's family was to pay for everything for a wedding, and they could not pay for anything.

Lanin shouldered her bag and moved for the door. "I will manage this on my own, Abish. Do not worry for me."

Indeed, Abish should let her go. Marriage to Belal was better for Lani than trying to figure out where to live next like the rest of them.

Timah glanced outside, and that was when Abish heard sounds coming from the back of the house. Two of the workmen were dismantling her little castle.

Why she was so hurt by it, she did not know. It was not as if she lived in it anymore. But the sight of it proved to her that this was not an accident. Jakob was doing this on purpose. It was not about money, but about attacking Haman's family and his legacy. Jakob must have felt that he had to destroy everything that Haman had left behind—everything that might prove that he could not measure up to his former employer.

Abish saw now that the workers looked through every corner and crevice of the house, taking out little treasures that Abish had long since forgotten about. They had already taken her mother's jewelry and any large items of value. In another hour, there would be nothing left for any of them. The workers were even taking their clothing.

She could not go with her mother to see Jakob. There was no time for that. She saw Timah walk out the door and prayed to the One True God that her mother would come home soon, no worse for wear. Considering what Jakob had shown of his true self, she was not sure that she could trust him not to harm her mother physically. It would be all too easy for him to claim that she was an old woman and had simply died of grief.

But she refused to think of that danger. There was too much to be done here.

Abish rushed up to her room. The men were not there yet. She thought as quickly as she could about what was most valuable. Her father's gifts could be sold. She needed those more than she needed her clothes. She pushed them into pockets, tied them around her waist under her skirts— anywhere she thought might hide them.

Then Abish hurried to her sisters and whispered to them to do the same.

"I have nothing," Gala said, looking upset and confused.

"Father didn't give us things like you," Jenan said unhappily.

There was no time for hurt or recriminations.

"Get whatever is most valuable. Clothes, trinkets, anything we might sell," she said as she pushed her sisters upstairs. At least they did not complain that she was too young to order them around.

When they came back, they showed her their favorite dresses and a few items that had only sentimental value. It was all Abish could do not to scold them that she'd said what they could sell—not what they wanted to remember of this place. They deserved to have whatever memories they could bring with them.

She had her father's vision and his understanding of the One True God. She carried the love of both of them in her heart. And she bore the weight of knowing that her mission to was to bring the true religion to the Lamanites. She had no idea how that would happen now that she was to be homeless and poverty-stricken—an unknown girl with no father to protect or provide for her. What kind of god treats those he loves in this way? Not the Lamanite gods, not in the stories that Abish had heard. But she had never felt the power of the Lamanite gods, either. She would have to think of all this through later.

Before dark, the house was cleaned out, the castle dismantled, and everything inside the house taken away. Even the remaining food was gone.

Abish was worried about her mother, but she dared not go after her and leave her sisters behind. She could already hear the whispers of the neighbors outside. They had gathered and begun to throw rocks, yelling that this was what Haman had always deserved, that he had stolen from the people of the city, and now his family had to give up the wealth that was never theirs.

It was after dark that Timah stumbled home. She was covered in dirt and bruised around her arms and face. She had scrapes on her arms and legs.

"Mother, what happened?" Abish asked.

Timah shook her head, unable to speak.

Abish ushered her mother upstairs, though there was no bed for her to lay on nor any blankets for her to find comfort in. Timah stretched out on the bare wood floor and stared up at the sky.

"Did you find Jakob? What did he say?"

Abish sent Gala to bring water from the well to her mother—at least the workers had not spoiled that.

Once Timah had drunk a little, she was able to speak. "I saw Jakob," she said.

"And?" Abish said.

"He told me that Haman had intended this. He said that I was to receive no portion because Haman had wanted him and Zara to have it all. Haman knew that to divide his business in any way would lead to it being weaker than he had built it to be." Timah's voice was monotone and dull as her eyes. The brief moment of energy she'd had when she decided to go see Jakob was gone now.

"What of Zara? Did you speak to her?" Abish asked. Surely her sister could not have known about this—or encouraged it. They were family.

But Timah wept at the mention of her daughter's name. Eventually she composed herself enough to say, "She would not speak to me. She ran away as if it was me she was afraid of, though I could see clearly it was Jakob. She fears doing anything against him, even in word or look."

There was nothing more to be done. They had no home. They would have only what they could take with them in the morning. They would somehow have to manage with that.

"We will go to Darius and Nesha," Abish said firmly. "They will take us in." It was a small comfort, but it was something.

Timah let out a sound of raw despair.

"What is it?" Abish demanded. "What's wrong?" She thought her mother might die then and there.

Gala and Jenan were also weeping. It took all of Abish's strength not to tell them to be quiet, to threaten them if they would not.

Finally, Timah wiped her face and said with that same dull tone, "I already saw Darius and Nesha. They rejected me, would not even look at me. Then Nesha came to me after and explained. She was shaking. Jakob threatened them, as well. They are not to speak to us, or Jakob will do to them what he has done to us."

"But—why?" Abish was bewildered. That made no sense. How would that help Jakob in any way? To be known as a man who sent women and children to live on the street?

"It is a message," Timah said, her fists clenched. "He wants everyone to know that Haman is no more and that we have no more power here. He is the only power."

There was little sleeping that night and much weeping, but it would be the last time for some years that they had even the energy to weep.

8

Lani married without any of her family there to celebrate. They heard the rumors about her being forced to marry in haste because she was already with child, but they could not defend her. They had no position to offer her. On the streets as they now were, it was all they could to stay alive in the chill of the night. They did not know what would happen if there was a storm or if it grew truly cold.

The first night none of them slept at all. They clung to each other near the marketplace, which was familiar and helped them to feel less frightened. But all of the sounds of the city seemed frightening now.

It was only in the day when they were finally able to sleep in a pile together, wrapped in each other's arms and legs. At least until the city guards came and woke them by prodding them with sticks as they did to all the poor in the city center. Abish suspected that they had been paid by Jakob to cause them further pain and anguish.

"He wants us to go to another city," Timah concluded.

"Maybe we should do exactly that," Abish said. They might have enough valuables left to buy something, a hovel, but that would be better than this life on the streets where no one dared so much as look at them because Jakob's threats had spread far beyond Darius and Nesha.

"No. I refuse to let him tell me where I will live," Timah said, with a surprising jut to her chin.

"Well, I'm going to marry," said Gala.

"Who?" Abish asked. She assumed Gala meant to one of the men she'd teased or flirted with before their father's death.

Gala slumped. "I don't know. It doesn't matter now. I will marry whoever asks me first. As long as he can give me a home and enough food to eat."

Despite the fact that Abish had some valuable items to sell, not one of the sellers she knew would buy them. And so none of the family had eaten for a full day, though Abish had insisted they all drink their fill at the well before they left the house the final time. It had not lasted long in their bellies, and Abish assumed that everyone else ached as much as she did.

"You must marry well," Timah said with a nod. "Your father would expect it.

Gala spat at her mother. "That is for my father, who brought me to this." She spat again. "And that is for you. I always hated you both, and now I know why. You were too stupid to understand how the world really works, and it is your fault we were led to this."

Abish never saw Gala again. She walked off, and Abish did not know if she married or not. She assumed that she had, or she would have returned. They would have eagerly seen her again, no matter what she had said to them.

But after Gala was gone, Jenan began to complain more fiercely than before. She would not listen to any of the rules her mother set for her. She spoke coarse words and began to spend time with the other beggars on the street.

"They are not for you!" Timah tried to tell her. "You must hold yourself above them."

"Above them? Mother, they are precisely where we are now. If anything, they are above us, for they know how to get money for food."

Jenan began to beg with the others. She wrapped a hand to pretend that she had damaged her fingers. Then she moved on to other disguises to get more sympathy. But whatever food it brought her, Abish and her mother saw none of it. She ate before she returned to them, if she returned to them, which was not often.

"She is too young to marry," Timah said in despair. But Jenan seemed to have no interest in marriage. Abish watched as her sister began to interest men at night, going off with them to their own places and return-ing hours later.

It disgusted her, but if Abish criticized Jenan, then what? Would Jenan leave them too?

So she said nothing and sold off the jewels and clothes as slowly and quietly as she could to those smaller sell-ers who had no business with Jakob. She knew they were cheating her but she had no choice. She had to eat, and she had to bring something back for her mother.

Her mother was losing weight rapidly, but it was her mind that Abish worried about the most. There were many mornings when she seemed to have forgotten that Haman had died or that they had been thrown out of their home. She would shout at Abish and tell her to bring her tea or some other delicacy that they could not afford now, and would hit Abish if she tried to explain why she could not do as she was asked.

Once Jenan came home in the midst of one of these attacks. She was wearing garish colors on her face and showed far too much bosom, but Abish said nothing about this. She looked disheveled and broken somehow, but she had eaten food at least. The smell of cheap wine was on her breath.

"Why do you let her treat you like that?" Jenan asked quietly after Timah had fallen asleep at last.

"She is my mother," Abish said. Surely that was the only explanation she needed to give.

"She was your mother. Now she is your child, but you never agreed to have her dependent on you," said Jenan. "Your real mother would never have wanted this for you. She would tell you to go and make your own way in the world, to think about yourself and your future."

Abish thought this might be true, and yet she did not want to leave the woman her mother had become. If she left now, what did that mean about her father's vision? He had seen that she had a mission to fulfill. He had told her about the One True God. He was the man who had been so changed that he had become a different person. If she turned away from her mother now, it would seem a rejection of her own destiny.

And besides, she still loved her mother. There were still good moments between them, even if they were not often.

"Where is Jenan?" Timah asked in one of her lucid moments.

"I don't know. Out there somewhere," Abish said with a wave of her hand into the streets.

"She thinks she is taking care of herself, but she does not understand the dangers. She was not raised here. She still thinks of the world the way a princess would," Timah said.

At the word "princess," Abish tensed. It was a painful reminder of all that she had lost when her father had died. She did not need to be a princess. She would put that part of her life behind her.

It would be easier if she could feel the love of the One True God again though. She had tried to pray many times since she had been on the streets. She had prayed in the dark while her mother shouted at her, and in the light when the guards had come to mock them or kick them and tell them to move along. But there seemed to be no answer from above.

One night Jenan came back to them more bruised than usual. This time she had also been cut badly across the face. When Abish saw the wound, she immediately wanted to take her sister to a healer.

"A healer?" Jenan laughed harshly. "There are no healers for women like me." She waved at her face. "It will heal, or it won't heal, and I will die. I hardly care anymore."

"We have one last jewel," Abish said, feeling in her skirt to make sure that it was still there, that it had not been lost or stolen. "We can use it for your face. Jenan, you must do something to care for yourself."

"No. I will not take the last jewel," said Jenan. She looked sad for a moment, and then she tensed again. "I won't have you remember me that way," she whispered.

"Jenan, what do you mean by that?" Abish asked.

Jenan would not answer for a while. Finally she said, "I should have listened to you from the first, Abish. I should have stayed with you and Mother."

"You did what you thought best," Abish said. "You can make a different choice now."

"No I can't. I am what I have now become. I can't go back. But I want you to know that I hope you have a good life. Somehow, Abish, keep that jewel. Think of the future. You were always the princess. I never knew until now that Father meant something about your character, not just his feelings for you. You were always different than the rest of us."

"I'm not," Abish insisted.

But Jenan said no more after that. She slept for a time, then ate a little of the food that Abish had found in the garbage of one of the stalls in the market. It was burned and half-rotten, but it was better than nothing.

In the morning Jenan was gone, and at first Abish did not think anything of it. She had probably woken to go back on the streets. She was probably staying with one of the men she earned money from.

But she did not come back. After a week Abish began to ask others on the streets if they had seen her sister. None of them had.

A month later her body washed up on the bank of the river, some distance from the bridge. Abish went to see the body, though it was so swollen the guards told her it was unrecognizable.

She knew immediately it was Jenan. It was Jenan's scarf around her neck and Jenan's birthmark on her shoulder.

She went home and wept. She did not know how to tell her mother, who kept asking where Jenan was. At last they went to bed, wrapped in their blankets, their stomachs growling from hunger pangs because Abish had not had time to find food that day.

The Lamanite gods said that those who died by their own hand were doomed to live another life in misery until they learned to accept suffering, but Abish could not believe this of her sister. Jenan made a mistake. She had been proud. But she did not deserve to be punished in another life. She deserved love and forgiveness, but there was only once source for that, and it was not the Lamanite gods.

So all through the night Abish cried to the Nephite God, demanding that she receive an answer. She wanted to know why this had happened and where her sister was.

And she demanded to know what kind of a God allowed a young woman who was not even fully grown to hurt herself because she had no desire left to live in a world that had hurt her too much.

The answer came only as Abish lay down at last, wondering if she should do the same that Jenan had done. It came not as a vision, but as a whisper.

"She is loved. She is home. You are also loved, Abish. And you will come home when it is your time."

"But why?" Abish wanted to know. "Why?" she directed her question at the heavens.

"She is loved. She is at home," came the answer again. There was no more than that, and Abish was tired enough that she stopped asking.

9

Abish didn't know how to tell her mother what had happened to Jenan, so she kept putting it off, day after day, until Timah came to her.

"You know where she is, don't you?" she asked, her eyes bright with anger. "Tell me the truth. If she has gone to another city and I will never see her again, I need to know. I need to stop looking for her face in the streets. I need to know that she is still alive, at least."

This made it even more difficult for Abish. Tears flowed from her eyes and her heart pinched in her chest. "Mother . . ."

Timah flung her hands wide. "Is she angry at me? Is that it? She thinks this is all my fault because I was too foolish to see who Jakob was when he first came to ask for Zara's hand in marriage? Is it because she thinks that I should go to a judge and ask for a portion back, based on what Jakob promised? Even if I have no proof of what her father wanted for us?"

"Mother, please," Abish choked out. "It is none of that."

"Then where has she gone? Is she with a man? Is she living with him without being married? Is she ashamed of herself and cannot face her mother?"

Her mother had known her daughter all too well, even after all the changes they had been through.

But Abish could still not bring herself to tell her mother the whole story. She would have to carry that burden alone. For now, she said, "She is dead, Mother. She fell into the river and drowned. I saw her body a few days ago and did not know if you could bear it."

She fell into her mother's arms and they wept together. There was some comfort in that.

"Oh my Jenan. Oh my sweet daughter. I wanted so much for you. You should have lived longer," her mother lamented. She tore at her hair until her head looked horribly bare. She ripped at her clothes as the wealthy people did in mourning, but they knew that they had other clothing to wear. Abish and her mother had nothing better to put on against the cold.

She had to be practical. "Mother, please stop. Jenan would not want you to do this. She is gone, but she must still be watching over us. Don't you feel her?" Abish knew that, according to the Lamanite's beliefs, Jenan's spirit should be reborn into another creature. But Abish did not believe that anymore. Now that she had felt her father with her, she believed that Jenan would still be herself in the next life, that she would be able to greet them again when they died.

"No, no, she is gone. Gone forever," Timah said. "I did not love her enough. She was never loved enough, by any of us."

Abish felt guilt for this herself. If she had never been born, Jenan would have been the youngest. She might have had far more of her father's attention, and her mother's. Maybe she would have been the "princess" of the family.

There were so many thing Abish wished now that she could go back and change from her childhood. She had been so spoiled, so selfish. She had treated all her sisters badly, and she had ignored Jenan as much as her parents had. Her only hope was that Jenan would forgive her some day.

Timah continued to mourn Jenan's death. She became known as the old woman who begged in the street during the day and wept all night long. People gave her coins because they felt sorry for her, and they had a bit more food, though Timah did not eat much of it. It was all Abish could do to get her mother to take a few bites before she began weeping.

There were times when Abish wondered if her mother was weeping more for Jenan or for her old life, when she was wealthy and secure, with her children all around her and her loving husband at her side. It was difficult for Abish too. But she did not allow herself to simply weep and give up. She had to keep going, for her mother's sake and for the sake of her father's vision. She had no idea how it might still come true, considering her current state, but the Nephite God had worked miracles before. She had to trust that things might change and that her life must have some use for her people.

On the first day of each week Abish watched for Nesha, who came with her twin daughters to the market. When they were very small, she tied them both to her back to keep her hands free so she could bargain more easily, and also so that she could carry home her things.

Though Abish knew that Nesha did not dare to speak to her openly, for fear word would get back to Jakob that she had disobeyed his command, she felt comfort in seeing one sister who did not despise her. Nesha would look Abish in the eyes, and though she never said her name, just knowing that someone remembered her meant everything to Abish. Without that look Abish might have wondered if her whole other life had been an imagined fantasy.

Then one day Nesha dropped something near Abish and Abish hurried to pick it up for her. But when she held it up her sister shook her head. "I dropped nothing," she said, and went on her way.

It took Abish a moment to realize that Nesha had meant for her to have this, and dropping it was the only way she could manage to give her sister and mother something without news getting back to Jakob.

Abish went back to the spot that she and her mother slept in—it was not a home, but at least they had found some fabric to put up over their heads to create a kind of shelter. Timah was there, asleep after a long night of weeping over Jenan.

Opening the wadded package in silence, Abish found three silver senines inside. It was so much money that she didn't know what to do with it. She was immediately afraid that one of the other beggars nearby would take it. How had Nesha managed to save so much? Would it make her life more difficult? Were she and her twins eating well?

Three silver senines was more than Abish had seen since her father died. She started to plan in her mind. How much would she need to rent a room somewhere? Should she save the money for food? Where could she put it for safekeeping? She would have to carry it on her person because she dared not leave it anywhere.

"Mother, good news!" Abish said, kissing her mother on the cheek.

Timah muttered something in her sleep but did not waken.

Abish went off to buy a special nut cake that her mother used to make at home, and which she said no one could make as well as she did. But when she tried to pay with the silver senine, the look she got made her worried that she would be accused of thievery. She took the change and the nut cake home with her and woke her mother up.

"Nesha gave us this," she said of the cake, not telling her mother about the money. She wasn't sure if Nesha would ever give them anything again, and she didn't want to raise her mother's hopes.

When she went to ask about renting a room in one of the nearby homes, however, she was turned away. As a beggar she was considered too "dirty."

But how could she get clean and stay clean if she did not have a home to stay in and a well nearby for fresh water to bathe in?

She washed in the cold, rushing water of the river and used the remains of the first silver senine to buy herself some fine clothing. Then she went back to ask about a room.

This time the excuse was that they had no empty rooms, though Abish was sure that they did.

They did not trust her. Why should they?

Abish went back to her mother, glad she'd said nothing about the coins. They were security for the future, but it seemed that a few senines of silver could not change anything now.

The next week Nesha came again. She didn't offer coins this time, but dropped a warm blanket, which Abish took back to her mother. Each week, Nesha dropped something for her mother and sister. It was the brightest, most hopeful part of Abish's life on the streets.

As for her other sisters, Abish caught glimpses of Zara with Jakob when she approached her father's old business. But she never saw Zara in the marketplace or on the streets alone. She began to suspect that Jakob was keeping his wife prisoner, making sure she never left their home. Was she being abused? Most likely, but there was no proof of that. And even if there were, a married woman could not get a judge to grant her a divorce for abuse alone.

After a year, Abish began to wonder why Zara was not with child. But she never grew heavy that Abish could see. Was it a curse or a blessing from the One True God? Abish didn't know.

Tamar, on the other hand, now had four children. Abish saw them in the marketplace, tagging after their mother. Tamar had a very harsh voice, and she scolded her children frequently. Worse than that, she hit them in public so that they wore bruises that looked very much like her own. It made Abish sick that her sister had become like her husband, that she had fallen so far.

Abish did not try to speak to Tamar. Even if she had been willing to share old stories, she turned away whenever she saw Tamar's children. She tried to muster sympathy for her sister, but she never could. Tamar should have protected her children, and not only did she fail to do so; she hurt them herself.

Old enough now to interest men, even if she was very thin, Abish refused the men who offered her a few coins and a tumble in the dirt—or even a visit to one of the cheap rooms in the city. Though she was desperate for a real bed, for a roof over her head at night, she could not forget what had happened to Jenan. She had the two silver senines and the remains of the third tied to her skirts, and that was security enough.

Lani and Belal had the least money of the married sisters. But Belal had no relationship to Jakob, and that made him freer to associate with Abish and Timah. He had no coin to spare them, and he lived in a one-room hovel as he worked from sunup to sundown for a merchant who traded with the Nephites. That meant that the merchant—and all those associated with him—were spit upon and called names whenever they entered the Lamanite marketplace. But people still bought their goods.

Abish sometimes wondered if the merchant himself, whose name was Lephi, was in fact a Nephite. His skin was not as fair as the slave Nephites she had seen, but he was lighter than many Lamanites.

If he was a Nephite, Abish wondered, could she talk to him about the One True God. She knew so little about how to worship properly. The God hadn't told her any of that in her experiences with Him. She didn't know what kinds of prayers to offer, or whether or not to buy special sacrifices to leave out, as she once had to the Lamanite gods.

She dared not ask Lephi openly, however. She could not afford to admit that she had changed her beliefs—not in the situation she was in now. She and her mother were too vulnerable. They could not afford be sent away from this city.

Occasionally Lani would invite Abish and Timah back to her one room to offer them a meal. It was usually when Belal had been given a bonus by the merchant for good work. Sometimes Belal was there, and sometimes he was not. If he was there, Belal would talk animatedly to Lani, as if he were afraid that Abish or Timah might say something and he would have to acknowledge them and think of something to say to them. When he wasn't there, Lani often let the silence stretch out for a long while.

"How do you do it?" she asked once when Abish and Timah got up to leave.

"Do what?"

"Not think about who you used to be, how you used to live?"

"I put it away," Abish said honestly. "It is there, but like a special gown. I don't wear it often. I want to keep it precious."

Lani let out a long breath and patted Abish's shoulder. "Oh, that's exactly what I do. It's like I was a different person then. I remember her life, and I live this life, and as long as they stay separate most of the time I do not feel too sorry for myself." She looked at Abish then as if she wanted to say she was sorry.

But what more could Lani do than she was already doing? There was no space in her home for her mother and sister, and she had a husband to take care of.

"Thank you for dinner. It is so good to see you, and to be able to talk to you." Abish thought of Nesha, who dared not say a word but gave silver senines. If she had the choice Abish would choose the luxury of speaking with her sister instead, but to say so sounded ungrateful. She knew Nesha was doing all she could.

The years went on. Timah grew older. Her hair was completely white, and she walked hunched over a stick for support—or with Abish at her side. She seemed less able to remember anything that had happened since Haman had died, and Abish grew tired of explaining all the terrible things to her. She let her sing to herself and pretend that her daughters were small again, all gathered around her and speaking too loudly or quarreling with each other, and that she was always—always—waiting for her husband to come home.

10

After Abish had been living on the streets for three years, she overheard a man being cheated at one of the cloth stalls at the marketplace. She'd seen the same merchant do the same thing to a dozen other customers and had told herself that she shouldn't intervene, that it would give her a bad reputation. But this time she could not let it go. The man being cheated was old and blind, and he held out a hand full of coins and asked the merchant to take what he'd said he was owed. The merchant took a coin worth ten times more than the good were worth.

"He cheated you," she said to the blind man. "He took the silver senine instead of the copper one."

"You beggar! Don't listen to her! She is in it for herself. She wants to take all your coins!" The merchant argued in return.

Abish felt the blind man began to tremble next to her. She tried to remain calm. "Just return his silver and he will go on his way," she said.

But the merchant's face grew red. "How dare you accuse me of anything! I am a good merchant. None of my customers has ever accused me of stealing."

Abish knew this was not true. She'd watched as the merchant had been accused of cheating one of his customers two days earlier. She hadn't intervened because she hadn't felt sorry for the customer, who seemed wealthy enough to ignore such a loss. But this was different.

"You will be cursed for this," Abish said. "You know the gods are watching." She assumed the merchant worshiped the Lamanite gods, but she also knew that the One True God was watching this all. She did not know what punishment from Him was like, but she was sure it would be severe for someone who stole from a helpless blind man.

The merchant came out of his stall and began to attack Abish physically with a large, wooden rod.

She ran away, pulling the blind man with her. "Come with me," she said, urging him forward through the streets. She knew the twists and turns better than the merchant did, so they escaped from him despite the fact that the blind man slowed her down.

"Thank you," said the blind man. "You are very kind to think of me."

But what had Abish really done for him? He had the cloth he'd purchased, but it was sweat-stained and dirty from their run through the streets. He had never received his coin back from the merchant, so she had done nothing for him at all except tire him out and ruin his cloth—and perhaps even make him an enemy of the merchant.

"I'm sorry," she said. She offered him one of her own silver senines from her skirt. "Take this." She pressed it into his hands.

"He gave it back?" said the blind man. "When did he do that? Why did he chase us if he accepted his blame?"

Abish had not thought of a suitable answer to this question, so she said, "It's a gift," she said. "Accept it as your due."

The blind man thought for a long moment. "It's your coin, isn't it?" he asked.

Abish sighed.

"Where in the world did a girl like you get a silver senine?"

Abish could not tell the truth, that it was from her sister. "I used to be wealthy," she admitted.

"And you've fallen so far?" said the blind man. "What happened?"

"My father died," Abish said. "And we were thrown into the streets, my mother and my sisters." She found herself unable to speak as she thought about Gala, whom she had not seen since the day she said she was going to be married, and Jenan, who had killed herself.

"Keep your coin," said the blind man. "You need it more than I do." He would not hear any different and he went off with a blessing to her from his god, the god of wind.

The next day, Abish stayed away from the marketplace, afraid that she would be harassed by the merchants. But when she dared to go back she found the merchants had not all taken the side of the one who had cheated the blind man. Some refused to look at her and spat at her if she came too close. Others seemed to look at her more kindly.

One even offered to pay Abish to run errands for him. It was the first job she'd ever had, and she had never expected to feel so thrilled about it. She'd had servants to run errands for her years ago, but she suspected they had never felt so eager to run through the streets as she did now. She did not earn any coins, but only goods the merchant knew he could not sell. But it was something, a beginning, a chance for her to prove she was useful.

After two months of working for the merchant he offered her a room to stay in. "To keep you safe through the winter," he said. "It is purely selfish on my part. I want you well enough to do more work for me."

"I don't think I can accept," Abish said, her head down. She did not want the man to think that she did not appreciate the offer.

He put up his hands. "I'm not trying to insult you. It is not a room in my house, but a room in one of the buildings I own. I would not make any assumptions about your virtue, I swear."

Abish's cheeks reddened. She had not meant that. She'd learned enough of his character, seen how he treated single women in the marketplace, to know that he would never do that to her.

"It's my mother," she explained. "I can't just leave her out here alone, and she is a beggar. She will not bathe or wear clean clothes. Sometimes she is loud and angry. I don't know that you would want to offer her a room with me when she does nothing for you."

The merchant hesitated for a moment, then said, "Would she be willing to stay inside if you were with her?" he asked.

"I think so," Abish said, hope beginning to spin in her heart. Were their days of being homeless about to end? Was this the beginning of the next stage in her life, when the promise from the One True God would come true and she would do something to save all her people?

The merchant sighed. "Then I will make sure the room is big enough for the two of you, and I will give you both my protection if there are any questions about her. Perhaps she will get well and begin to care about herself again."

He showed Abish the room that night. It was so tiny that it did not remind her of her home or her castle from her life before. But it was clean and dry, and it would be warm through the winter. "Thank you," she said. "I will be happy to accept this for myself and my mother."

She had hoped that she could simply show her mother the room, but it was not that easy. It took a week of coaxing Timah, showing her the room again and again, then convincing her to fall asleep there only to wake to find that her mother had gone back to her familiar place on the streets.

Abish prayed to the One True God to express her gratitude the morning she woke to find her mother still with her. Now she did not have to worry about being overheard by others and reported to the guards as a Nephite spy. She thought about the rumors of war she had heard, and she wondered if that was what she was to save her people from.

Some weeks later a man stopped her in the streets as she was running by and asked her for directions to her father's business.

"Why do you want to go there?" she asked suspiciously. "I've heard that it's the best place to buy quality bricks and that the workers are treated well," he said.

She did not realize that she held such a grudge against Jakob, but she would not lift a finger to do anything that might help him. "That is not what I've heard," she said bluntly.

The man's eyebrows went up, and Abish saw then that he had an old wound across his face. It puckered his cheek and his eyes. The wound must have happened when he was a child, though, because he was not very old.

"Is there someone else I should go to?" he asked. "For building?"

Abish thought of her father's competitors. She didn't like any of them particularly, but one of them was known for being fair, even if he was often rude.

"Go to Nagoth's. He is down that way." She pointed. "Turn left at the stone pillars and then go six hundred paces toward the mountains."

"Nagoth?" the scarred man echoed. "You're sure he's better than Haman?"

"Haman is dead," Abish said bluntly. "And he was my father. No one was a better man or a brick maker than my father, but Jakob owns the building business now, and he is cruel."

The scarred man stared at Abish for a moment and then looked away. "I am sorry for your loss. Is there anything I can do for you?"

"No," Abish said. "But do something for Nagoth and his workers. And spread the word about Jakob. If he hears that his bad reputation is ruining his business, perhaps he will change." Though Abish did not think he would change in his heart, at least he could treat his own workers better. She dared not hope that he would invite her and her mother back to their home or give them what he had promised her father.

Even if Jakob had a vision from God, as her father had, Abish felt convinced that he would not change. She did not understand why some men had visions and some did not, but she thought that the One True God knew His own. Or perhaps they all did have visions ,and most people simply ignored them because they weren't convenient. It was never convenient to change your heart and admit your mistakes in the past.

"I met your father only one time, but he struck me as the best and kindest of men. Honest and truthful with a good heart. He gave money at the end of every day to the poor here in the marketplace, did you know that?" he asked.

It felt strange to be talking to someone about her father after spending so much of her time trying to push away her past life. Abish struggled against tears. "I didn't know that," she said. It was hard to conjure an image of her father without pain.

"I went with him once, and he knew many of them by name. They loved him," said the scarred man.

"And I loved my father very much as well," Abish whispered, then looked away. She couldn't move on just yet. She didn't trust her legs.

The scarred man said, "I was one of the poor he helped. I was a beggar in the streets for many years. I don't remember my parents, but I suspect that they hurt me and I ran from them." He gestured at his face. "If not for your father, I would never have learned a trade and become the man I am now."

"That's good to hear," Abish got out.

"I sometimes work with the king himself now, advising him on his business dealings and helping him think of new ways to deal with the poor. I must thank your father for all of that," said the scarred man.

Abish nodded, overwhelmed. She'd focused on her own life as a child and hadn't thought about what her father might have done for others with his wealth. It only made her sadder that he was gone, and angrier that Jakob had taken his place.

"So when I ask if I can do anything for you, I mean it. I owe you through your father. Please, let me give you something." He held out some coins.

Abish stared at them. There was a time when she would have felt obliged to take them, for her mother's sake. But they had a room now. They had more than one piece of clothing to wear. They could bathe and wash clothes and eat simple foods that they prepared themselves. Their life was so much better than it was when they'd been on the streets.

She shook her head. "Give them to someone truly poor," she said. "There are so many of them." And when she saw them, she always wished there was some way she could help them. It hurt to leave them behind. That was the one thing she had not anticipated about improving her own life—that she would feel torn about those she left behind in poverty.

"I've offended you. You feel I'm being patronizing," said the scarred man.

"No, it's not that," Abish said. "I just feel blessed with what we have already. My mother and I are well." And she could do nothing anymore for Jenan. Or Gala, wherever she was, if she was still alive.

"You have a job?" the scarred man asked.

It was none of his business, really, but Abish nodded. "I work for a merchant. In fact, I should get back to his stall now. He sent me to bring a message to one of his workers." She pointed in the direction she had been headed when the man asked her advice.

"Go, then," said the scarred man. "Wait! Tell me your name."

Abish hesitated.

"My name is Atir," he said.

"I'm Abish," she said.

"Good to meet you, Abish. I hope to see you again."

Abish did not expect to see Atir again. If it was true that he worked with the king, he must take care not to be seen with someone as lowly as her.

But the next day, he found her at the merchant's stall. "You're the youngest, aren't you?" he said. "Your father's princess?"

He had meant it lightly. Abish could see the smile on his face, as if it were a joke. But the words made her heart clench. She was so far from that now that it was hard to laugh at the title.

"Excuse me," she said, and walked away from him.

He did not appear the next day, or the next. She had treated him rudely, and she thought she was rid of him. What did she care? It was not as if she wanted to see him again. He would only remind her of all the things she had lost.

But he appeared at the end of the week. And this time he waited for her politely until she was finished with all of her errands for the day. He waited for six hours, in the hot sun, without ever leaving to get himself a drink or food.

"You're going to fall over," she said at the end of the day, as she offered him her own water pouch.

He took a sip and returned it to her. "As kind as your father was," he said with a smile.

How could he smile after she had made him wait for so long? "If I told you that I never want to see you again, that you are bothering me, what would you do?" she asked.

He looked stricken. "I'm sorry," he said. "I did not mean to make you feel pressure. I only wanted to show you that I was willing to wait. But I will leave now if you wish." He was already taking a step away from her.

It was all the answer she needed. She pulled him back to her side and offered him her water pouch again. "Tell me about my father," she said, giving herself this one brief moment to think about what she had lost.

Atir's eyes grew misty and he seemed to have gone far away. "I stole from him. I picked his pocket, though it almost seemed as if he wanted me to do it. He was moving slowly, and I could see the coins jangling so close. He had no belt for them. Or at least they were not in his belt."

"And then what?" Abish said.

"He chased after me, and I was terrified. I knew he was a wealthy man. He could call the guards and have me beaten. Or worse, thrown into prison. No one would care where I had gone. I had no family." His hands had tightened into fists in memory of his fear.

"But he didn't?" she asked.

Atir shook his head. "He offered me a job. He said that if I would come and tell him who was on the streets and needed help most, he would hire me to take them what I thought they would accept. I did not believe him at first, but he was as good as his word. My only job was to give his money to those in need in a way they did not find objectionable."

Abish's heart felt full. Sometimes it was hard to remember her father's loss, but Atir made it easier. It reminded her that he had truly become a good man when the One True God had touched him. He had chosen to help all those he could find, to see in them all the face of the Nephite God.

"He was a good man," Atir said.

"Yes," Abish said.

"I didn't know that he had died. I was away for a time. In Nephite lands. Your father had encouraged me to take a chance at seeing the world, and I—I am sad now that I was not here to say goodbye." His voice was choked with emotion.

Abish put her hand over his and held it. "Thank you. You don't know what a gift it is to share memories of him. My mother—she isn't always aware of what happened. She thinks he is still alive, and that makes it difficult for me."

Just last night, Timah had attacked Abish and insisted that they must go home. Abish had chased her across the city until they found out what had happened to their old home. It had become a stable for cattle. Goats and sheep were in her bedroom. It was a stupid use for a home that must have been more valuable to Jakob than this. But it was a way for him to get back at them, to say what he thought of them. And of Haman.

"I wish you would let me do something for you. A home? A better room, at least?"

Abish shook her head. She did not want to be a burden to him. Nor did she want to do anything that might offend the merchant she worked for.

"I could find you a better job—one that pays in real coin," suggested Atir.

"Thank you, but no," Abish said. She was happy with what she did now.

"Even if I could find you a place in the king's own palace? Wouldn't that make you feel safer?" Atir pressed.

Abish felt the pain to her heart again. The idea of being a servant in the king's palace, where once she had been the princess in her own—no, that was too much. "Please, stop. You don't need try to repay me for what my father did for you."

"I'm sorry. You think it would be painful to work for the king. I should have thought of that," Atir said. "Forgive me."

Abish nodded. The pain was already subsiding.

"I used to envy you, when I saw you and your sisters at your home. You had all the love and attention that I never had. You had parents who loved you. And you—you were so beautiful. All of you." He was staring at her in a way that made it clear that he was speaking of her specifically.

"Much good it does me now," Abish muttered. As far as she could tell it only made her more likely to suffer unwelcome attentions in the marketplace.

"My first memories are of being laughed at in the street for my face." He waved at his scar. "I don't know where I came from. I have no family. Your father was the only father I ever had. I worshiped him."

The word "worship" made Abish think of the One True God. And then she remembered that Atir had said that he had visited the Nephites. Did he know of their God?

"What did you learn from the Nephites?" she asked.

Atir looked around before he answered her, clearly worried about being overheard. "They are not as bad as we think they are. They have families, just like we do. They fall in love and marry like we do."

It was a bland answer, and not nearly enough for her curiosity, no more than that, her need to know the truth. "But their God?" Abish pressed.

"Yes, their God is different. I think—I think that their God speaks to them individually. He gives them counsel when they need correction and love when they despair."

"Do you think they are better than we are because of their God?" Abish asked boldly.

Atir looked around again and spoke in a whisper. "Not better than we are, no. I think when they turn against their God they are much worse. I don't think I would choose to be one of them, but I respect them now that I've seen them."

Abish wanted to hear more about Atir's experiences with the Nephites. "Did my father ever tell you what he thought of the Nephite God?" she asked.

"No," Atir said, surprised.

Someday, Abish thought, she might tell him. If she learned to trust him enough. For now she said, "Would you like to come in and meet my mother?"

11

Atir had a gift with Timah. He never corrected her if she was in a different time or place. She sometimes called him "Haman" and wanted him to kiss her, and he obliged without complaint. Other times, she thought he was her brother "Jezor," and told him all the things he had done wrong and sometimes swatted him in anger. Atir would be Jezor, as well.

"I'm sorry she treats you like that," said Abish, who wished that her mother could understand who Atir really was—and who he might soon become in her family, if Abish had her wish.

"It's not as if she can hurt me. She has no more meat on her bones than a bird," Atir said, laughing gently.

Abish winced at the implied criticism.

"She won't eat," she said. She spent hours a day trying to get her mother to eat more, but she could not stay home all day long. And even if she did, her mother slept so much now that she didn't have time to eat as much as she needed to.

The truth was, Abish knew that Timah was dying, but refused to allow herself to weep over it. Her mother had lived a good life. She had known both joy and sorrow. She had been loved, truly loved, as few women ever were. And she had been touched by the One True God when Abish was born. What more than that could any woman wish for?

"I think all she wants is to find your father somehow," Atir said softly.

Abish nodded, thinking about what would happen when Timah died. "He will be glad to have her return to him as well, I'm sure," she murmured.

Atir hesitated a moment before saying, "Do you believe that? What the Nephites believe? That there is another world after this one where we are as we are now, only immortal? Where we will be with our families again?"

"I think I do," Abish said. It was a belief that had kept her going after her father and Jenan had died. She would hold to it even more firmly once her mother was gone.

"Then what about me?" Atir said. "I don't know who my family is. I have no memory of them. All I have left of them is this scar." He pointed to his face. "And I don't know that the parents who did this to me are the parents I want to live with again in another world."

"Oh." Abish hadn't thought of this. She'd assumed that everyone would be comforted by the idea of meeting their family again in the other world. "But you don't know how that happened, though, do you?"

"It didn't happen from being kissed too often," Atir said drily.

"No." Abish held his hand. "I'm sorry," she said. "You deserve the best of all families, and I'm sure the One True God will find one for you, even if it isn't your own."

Atir let out a breath and seemed to grow more fragile. He spent most of his day making himself look invulnerable, but when he came to her it was different. He let himself take off his armor and become real.

"I used to try to make myself remember my parents. I don't know how old I was when they left me in the streets. I don't know when I was born or what my heritage is. Maybe I'm a Nephite myself. I will never know. My parents could have been robbers coming to the city to kill Lamanites, to cause a war, or simply to pillage and rape."

Abish shivered at this. There were so many stories about how terrible the Nephites were. Little girls were warned to run away from any Nephite monster, to scream and call out, because they would be killed immediately and their bodies desecrated—perhaps eaten. Nephites were the nightmares of most Lamanite children. But the truth was that Abish had never met a Nephite in person.

"When I tried to remember, it would make me sick. I would vomit and have headaches for days. That made me think that there must be something there, if only I could get at it. The truth, whatever it is, is so horrible that my mind is somehow protecting me from it."

"Or it's too old for you to remember, and you are just hurting yourself trying," Abish said.

"Yes. I hate the idea that I'm too weak to remember the truth."

"Not too weak. That's not what I meant. I just meant— it's useless."

"Ha," Atir said. "It's all too likely that my father killed my mother in a drunken fight, and I was stupid enough to try to save her, so he tried to kill me too. I've seen enough children like that to know how often it happens. And if the Nephites are right about the other world and us living with our families, then I don't want to be forced to live with them." He shuddered at this.

"Of course not," Abish said. The One True God of love that she knew would never force any child or wife to live with an abuser.

"But if I must have a new family that I've never known before—is that truly a glory to look forward to?"

"It is if they're a new family you know and love. Like us," Abish said suddenly. She knew it was forward, but she said it anyway. "Atir, if you want it, my father will be your father and my mother your mother. My sisters will be your sisters, if you'll take them. You might prefer some to others. I know I do. But they come all together, it seems."

Once the words were said, she was pulsing with fear of his response. Did he think of her this way at all? He'd been so kind to her, but perhaps she had misunderstood it all. He might only think of her like a sister, and not the way she had begun to think of him.

Atir shook his head. "Your father died before he knew me. Who knows how he would feel about me? And your mother is not herself now, though I think she likes me. As for your sisters, they seem to be a mixed blessing." He was not even smiling at this. He looked pale and unsure.

"Maybe you have sisters of your own. Or worse, still, brothers. And they are out there waiting for you to come home to them. They might be just as annoying as mine," Abish said, growing more unsure every moment. Would she have to give up her love for Atir as well as everything else she had given up in her life?

"I used to think about that too," Atir said quietly. "For years, as I was growing up, I imagined that this man on the street, or that one, might be my brother. I looked for similarities, staring at my face in the water whenever I could to memorize its features. An uncle, a cousin, a grandfather. I wanted to find anyone I could. But when I think about it, I wonder—if I had other family members, why did they not find me? Why did they never look for me? The city is not so big that they could not have found me if they had wanted to."

Abish's heart ached for Atir again. "Atir, I think that the Nephite God would want you to be with those who love you. In this world and the next, but if that's not me and my family—" She stopped because then Atir was kissing her fully on the mouth. It was the first time they had kissed, and she wanted to enjoy the moment. She wanted to pull back and try again, to make sure that she remembered it.

But Atir's kiss grew deeper, more urgent, and his hands went around her chest and held her tightly to him. His breathing was ragged, and she felt urgency in him. They were in love. What difference would it make if they were married officially or not? Many of the poor Lamanites simply began living together.

But Atir pulled himself back, looked away, and then shook his head. "Now I'm sorry," he said.

"Mother wouldn't mind," Abish said, nodding to the room behind them where she slept most nights at her mother's side. She worried that her mother would wander off, so she never slept very deeply, and the bedding was nothing like what she had once had. But it was a home, and she valued that. She wanted Atir to be part of it.

"Your father would," Atir said.

"My father is dead, as you just pointed out," Abish said. And she wanted Atir to be her husband in truth, right now. She had seen so little love for so long.

"And if the Nephites are right, I will meet him again in the next world and have to explain myself to him," Atir said. He turned to face her, his eyes glowing with shame and hunger at the same time.

"Once we give him some grandchildren, I'm sure he won't mind anymore," Abish tried to tease.

But Atir would not hear of it. "I have no other family, Abish. You are right about that. The only thing that makes sense to me is that you will be my family. You and our children and your parents and your sisters. I want to do right by them."

Abish didn't argue with him anymore. She loved Atir because he was a good man, because he wanted to do right by her. So they would wait. For how long?

"I will ask the king if he can give us special permission," Atir announced. "He can waive the fees and make the announcements in all the city tomorrow if he chooses to do so."

"The king?" Abish was nervous. She didn't know the man, though Atir said that he was good and kind. As the leader of all the Lamanites he had the power to stop their marriage, if he chose. What if he did not like her? What if he thought Atir deserved better?

"I will take care of it all. Don't worry, Abish. We will be married soon." Atir kissed her gently on the forehead and left her that night with her mother.

In the morning a miracle happened, and Timah was herself for a single hour. "That man who was here last night," she said.

"Yes, Mother?"

"He loves you," Timah said. "What is his name?"

"Atir," Abish said, watching to see if her mother was about to begin raging about robbers and rapists as she sometimes did.

"Ah, yes. How long have you been seeing him?" Timah asked.

"A little less than a year."

"Well, you are old enough to marry now," Timah said.

Tears sprang into Abish's eyes. "Yes," she said.

"And your father is gone, so I suppose I am the only one who must give consent."

"Do you give consent, Mother?" Abish asked.

Timah's mouth twisted. "After the men I have given consent to marry my daughters, I'm not sure that my opinion matters. If he were a fool or a demon, I could not tell. But if you love him then you must make your own choice in the matter," she said heavily.

"I do love him. And he is neither fool nor demon. If you knew all about him, Mother, you would love him as I do." Abish had never spoken such true words. She felt as if her heart had swollen in her chest.

"Tell me about him then. Tell me why he is better than other men." Timah smiled a little and seemed more like her mother than she had been in years.

And for the next hour, Abish told her mother all about Atir, about the first time she had met him, and about all the kind things she had seen him do. She told her mother about Atir and her father's first meeting, about the king, about the poor, and about Atir's scar and his lack of family.

"I like the idea that your father met him," Timah said. "He would have wanted to know that his daughter was marrying a man worthy of her."

"I cannot imagine being happier if he were the king himself," Abish said. No man had ever treated her more like a princess, not even her father.

"Princess," her mother said softly, closing her eyes and beginning to sing a lullaby that Abish remembered from her childhood. Her mother was gone after that, back to her confused state, but Abish prayed thanks to the Nephite God that she had been allowed that one hour. It made up for the fact that Timah did not come to the wedding itself.

Atir did not return for more than a week, and though Abish tried to assure herself that he loved her and must have his reasons, she was afraid that he would not return, that she had pressured him, or that he was ashamed of the way that she had kissed him in return.

When he did come back, she felt such relief that she nearly broke down crying. "It is so good to see you," she said, and put her arms out to embrace him.

But he held back. "Are you alone?" he asked.

"My mother is here," Abish said, nodding to her mother's bed.

Atir kissed her on the cheek, but lightly, like a brother to a sister. "I have good news," he said.

"Yes?" Abish was afraid to let herself believe that this could happen. She could be happy again, even if she did not think that her father's vision of her future would come true the way he'd wanted it to.

"King Lamoni has given us permission to marry at the end of this week." He was full of light at the announcement, and Abish forgave him for frightening her so badly in his absence.

"This week?" she said, her own excitement barely contained.

"And more than that, Abish, he has lent us the palace itself. Of course, we cannot marry in the great hall as his daughters or sons will, but we may have the courtyard, and our guests can come to the back of the palace as servants would." He used his hands to gesture as if the walls around them belonged to the king. "The palace kitchens will provide some food for us, and the king will offer some of his own wine. What do you think of that?" he turned and looked deeply into her eyes, as though afraid that she might disapprove of what he was offering.

But it was all more than Abish could possibly have hoped for. She threw herself into his arms, and they cried and laughed and danced together until her mother complained that they were being too loud.

It wasn't until the next day that she worried about everything else, and she spilled it out to Atir in one burst. "I don't think we can marry in the castle, though you must thank the king for the offer," she said.

"Why ever not?" Atir asked, confused.

She looked away. "I fear it would only be embarrassing for us and for the king. After all, we have no guests to invite. My mother cannot be there. My sisters will not come. I have no proper dress to wear. I will not know what to say or how to act with the king or with anyone else there. Please, tell the king thank you, but we must marry in the marketplace or somewhere else." She broke down, weeping.

Atir assured her that all would be well, that he would make sure of it, wherever they were married.

"No, it can't be well. We can never be married, I think. I'm doomed to unhappiness," Abish said, though she knew later that she'd exaggerated and was embarrassed at her own overflow of emotions.

Atir returned the next day and told her that King Lamoni had sent the princess's own seamstress to come that very night and help her select fabric and patterns for a wedding dress. As for guests, the king had his own ideas for that, and if her sisters would not come they would be refusing an invitation from the king himself.

"So you see, everything will be taken care of. You will truly have a wedding in the palace, and the king himself will be there to give you away in your father's place. He has heard all about your father from me, and he insisted that he be allowed the honor."

"Are you sure?" Abish asked, trying to let go of her last fear that this was all too much goodness for her, that somehow it would all be taken away at the last moment.

"Of course I'm sure." Atir kissed Abish thoroughly, then swung her around in his arms. The look in his eyes was enough to make her stop worrying and give into the feeling of boundless happiness she felt with him. The One True God seemed to have decided it was time at last for her life to change again.

12

The day of the wedding was bright and beautiful, though it was a cold fall day. There was wind blowing all around, and Abish was glad she had chosen cloth from the royal seamstress that was thick and warm. The dress had arrived the night before, package neatly in red ribbons and by one of the king's own messengers. Abish had taken it out to show her mother.

"Is it for Tamar's wedding?" Timah asked.

"No, Mother, it is for my wedding. To Atir. Do you remember him?" she asked gently.

Her mother laughed in a high tone, like a child. "You are too young to marry, little Abish. Of course it must be for Tamar. She will look lovely in it."

When Abish put on the dress her mother called her "Tamar" and told her that she had been wise to listen to her father's advice to wait to marry until she was older.

The king sent a woman over later that morning to watch over her mother during all of the wedding celebrations. The woman looked to be Timah's own age, and they spoke of things that Abish had never heard of from long ago— stories of the long ago Nephite war and the brave men who had saved the kingdom from the Nephites then.

Abish left her mother in peace. She had intended to walk to the palace, holding her skirts up so that they did not get dirty, but there was an escort and a pallet waiting, and they insisted that the king had commanded them to carry her. So Abish had the strange experience of being lifted above the four men's heads and carried to the palace while all those in the streets around her stared and pointed. She felt like a princess indeed.

Her four sisters were all there to greet her. Only Jenan, who had died, and Gala, whom Abish had no location for, were missing. Though they were afraid of Jakob, it seemed that they were more afraid of the king.

Abish was surprised to see Jakob himself, at Zara's side, standing to greet her as she was let down from her pallet.

Atir was waiting for her there, and she hurried to his side. He was dressed as finely as she was, like a king. His tunic was made of wool, and there were jewels sparkling in the hat on his head. Borrowed clothing that would have to go back to the king, no doubt, but her memories of this day were so sweet that she would not regret that. This was precisely the wedding she had dreamed of as a young girl.

King Lamoni himself greeted them as they stepped into the courtyard. He was tall and handsome and dressed in jewels and animal skins atop fine red robes. He acted as father to both Atir and Abish, walking them to the front where the king's own priest waited to marry them offi-cially before the Lamanite gods.

It wasn't until that moment that Abish thought about wanting to be married in the Nephite way. She didn't know much about how the Nephites practiced their religion, but if she believed in the One True God and not the many gods, it was strange not to have him invoked at their wedding. She looked at Atir and could see that he knew what she was thinking. But what could she say? Tell the king that she wanted a Nephite priest instead? Of course, she couldn't do that. This was a true marriage, as much as she would get in this life anyway.

"Give us your blessing, One True God," she whispered, and then she moved forward. She and Atir knelt in front of the priest, who called for a goat to be sacrificed to the gods to bring happiness to this marriage. She and Atir both had to drink from the same cup of the goat's fresh, warm blood. Then the priest declared them married before the people, and there were shouts and cheers from the guests the king had brought, though Abish heard nothing from her own sisters.

Afterwards, the palace kitchens brought out so much food and of such richness that Abish could only eat a little of it. She went around and spoke individually to her sisters. Tamar and Laman were first, as Tamar was the eldest.

"It is good to see you again," Abish said. She introduced Atir. "I hope you and your children are well." Tamar did not have any visible bruises, but her smile seemed strained.

"Very well," said Tamar. "You must tell the king how happy we are that you are married. We are so very proud of you." She looked to her husband, as if for approval.

"I will gladly come to visit you here," said Laman. "I believe I would have much to offer the king if he knew me better."

Of course, they thought that Atir would allow them new opportunities to increase their social position and their wealth. Abish was furious that this was the first time she'd been allowed to see her sister in years, but she said nothing and simply smiled in return.

"I'm sure that you will be happy to come to share dinner with us," she suggested.

"Yes, yes," said Laman. "Any time you choose."

Tamar looked ill at the thought. Abish could not understand why. Did her sister hate her now?

"Tamar hates to be away from the children, but of course, she will come," Laman said. "If you ask her."

"Perhaps we could visit you instead, then," Atir said.

Tamar looked even more distressed at this, her lips thinning and her face going pale. "Of course," she said aloud.

Abish wanted to help her sister more, but she did not know how. Would the king's favor make Laman treat her better? She could only hope so.

Nesha and Darius were next. Nesha was weeping and embraced her sister tightly. "I am so happy for you. I am so glad to see you here, where you belong." Nesha had never said such a thing before. She had been as jealous as the other sisters were, but perhaps she thought that Abish's suffering had earned her this.

"Thank you for all you've done for me and our mother," Abish said. "I will never forget that."

Darius said nothing, but patted Nesha gently, which made Abish convinced that he had known what Nesha was doing all along and had encouraged her.

Then it was time to greet Jakob and Zara. Jakob was all smiles, thumping Atir on the back and nodding at Abish. Zara looked angry, but she offered her sister a gift wrapped in expensive silk.

"Thank you," Abish said. Should she open it now?

"Go on," said Jakob. "You will be thrilled to see this."

Abish opened it and caught her breath at what she saw. It was one of the treasures she had hidden long ago in her castle basement: a gift from her father, a stuffed doll that had been nearly loved to death.

"We thought you would like to pass it along to your own child in time," said Jakob. "A reminder of your father."

His men must have taken this when they had taken her home and sent her away. It felt less like a gift and more like a further reminder of his power over her, and it infuriated her that he would bring this to her wedding, in front of the king.

"I think that Abish is overcome with emotions," Atir said, trying to smooth over the moment when Abish went tense with anger. "But I'm sure she thanks you for your gift."

Abish met Zara's eyes. Was her sister part of this, or was she an unwilling participant in her husband's cruelty?

She let out a long breath. She could not tell. She thought that her sister had now spent too many years trying to play a part in order to survive. Abish would not blame her. And truly, she was glad to have this gift back. She had not thought of it in years. She had not taken it with her because it could do nothing to keep them alive. She would be glad to give it to her own child, even if Jakob would have no part in that story. He did not deserve any credit for saving her father's doll.

"If the king has any building projects in mind, you must give him a recommendation for my business," said Jakob. "I will give him the best price, and I can promise that the work will be up to your father's own standards."

Jakob was the last man that Abish would recommend to the king for any reason, business or personal. But she did not want to spoil her wedding day by saying this aloud. She just wanted Jakob to go.

"I'm sure Abish will always remember you and all you have done for her," Atir said carefully, tightening his grip on Abish's arm.

"I'm sure that we have much in common. You must come to visit us often. I don't know how we happened to have been separated for so many years. Your sister has always wished to have you as one of her companions," Jakob said.

"Yes, of course, Abish," Zara said. "I missed you terribly. And Mother?" There was a faint note of question at the end. She did not know if her own mother was alive or dead.

Abish had pity on her sister for a moment. "Mother is ill, but she is alive still." If Zara ever bothered to visit, she could find out the truth about her mother's mind, but now was not the time for that.

Finally, Abish and Atir greeted Lani and Belal. Lani was wearing what looked like a borrowed dress. It had certainly not been made by the king's own seamstress, and it fitted her poorly, but it shone in the light and it made her look less thin than Abish knew she was.

Abish embraced her fragile sister and kissed her cheek.

"I'm so happy for you," Lani whispered. "You deserve all of this."

"I don't, but thank you for coming. And for loving me."

"I wish I could have done more—" Lani began.

"No," Abish said. "You did what you could. You have your own children to care for now." Lani's belly looked like it was growing again, and Abish promised herself that she would send something over to help her. Food or coins or something.

Belal shook Atir's hand. "Welcome to the family. You have one of the best parts of it, I think. Not all the parts are good I fear." He glanced toward Jakob.

"You are one of the other good parts of it," Atir said.

Lani and Belal promised to go over and visit Timah before they went home. She was the only sister who seemed to want to know where their mother was living, Abish noted.

After the wedding guests had gone the king invited Abish and Atir to tour the palace. It was not something Abish felt she could say "no" to, so she went.

They saw the king's fabulous baths, the library where he kept some of the ancient records from the days of Laman and Lemuel, the first brothers. There were also some documents from those who had lived in this land before the Lamanites had arrived and samples of flowers that no longer grew there, animals that had died out, and rock fossils of long dead animals no one had ever seen.

King Lamoni also showed them the palace kitchens, which were so large that Abish's head swam. She thought the whole marketplace might fit inside of this one room. There were herbs here she had never heard of, dozens of racks of meat, ready for cooking, and six ovens for cooking bread that were in constant use. It was hot and delicious smelling and overwhelming.

Then the king introduced Abish to his five daughters and his six sons. The queen was in bed with the young-est, who was only a few days old. The younger princesses wanted to ask questions about the wedding. The older ones seemed more bored. Abish wondered if any of them would make as good a ruler as their father was. Did the children of the wealthy always end up selfish and cruel? If she had not experienced poverty herself, she did not think she would have become kind. She would never have seen the value in Atir's character either. She would have been ashamed to marry him, seen it as lowering herself. But, of course, she had been so very wrong.

At last, the king walked them to the gate at the end of the gardens. The smell of the gardens was nearly as intoxicat-ing as the basement wine cellars underneath the kitchen, dug into the stone foundation of the palace from hundreds of years before.

King Lamoni turned and said graciously, "Atir, you are a gift to our kingdom. I am pleased that you continue to help the poor. I do not know your wife well, but I know that she must be worthy of you. You would not love a woman who did not have a heart as big as your own."

Abish blushed at this.

Now the king turned back to Abish with a wry expression. "You have met my daughters, and I think you already see the problems that I see in them every day. You also had six sisters who lived a privileged life. But my daughters have never been forced into poverty as your sisters have."

He grimaced. "They have known luxury and ease all their lives, and now they look down on others. I am embarrassed as a king that I have not taught them better. I have not known who might be better than their own mother, who is a good woman but overwhelmed with so many children. May the gods bless us with more." He made a gesture toward the trees, which Abish took to mean that he favored the Lamanite gods of the trees.

"I'm sure she is a wonderful queen," Abish got out, knowing that her words were completely inadequate for all the king had done for her and Atir.

The king nodded to Atir. "Now I have met Abish, and I want her to work in the palace so that my daughters will see her example. You grew up in wealth and understand the problem in a way that no one else could. They will respect you for the graces you learned from your father, and they will see how hard you work even so. What do you have to say? Will you come to work in the palace as a servant or is that too lowly a position for you?"

Nothing the king could have said would have shocked Abish more. "I—I—" she stuttered.

"You need time to think about it. I apologize. I should not have asked you such a question on the day of your marriage. I will give you a week, shall I? Then you can answer me and tell me if you will help us all tame my daughters, yes?" The king had a way of speaking that made it difficult to refuse him. Even if he had not been a king, he could have earned a living as a storyteller or an actor.

Or as a thief, Abish thought. But that was not all. He was sincere in his wishes, and it was difficult to refuse him now that she had met the daughters and seen the problem for herself.

"I have work already," Abish said. "A good job. A business that protected me for many years." She could not imagine telling the man who had saved her life and her mother's that she could no longer work for him.

"Of course you are loyal to such a man. But if I were to pay for your release from that obligation, would you consider it then?" He named a sum that made Abish gape at him. "More than that?" he asked.

"It is not merely the money, great King," Atir said. "She feels an obligation that goes beyond that. This man helped her when no one else would."

"But he does not need her now, surely. Is it her mother? I would make a room for her in the palace, for all of you, of course. And there would be other servants to help watch over her. She would be far safer here than where you live now, I think," the king said.

He made it difficult to say no, but Abish said that she would think about it and give an answer at the end of the week.

Then she and Atir went home to her mother, to the tiny room that had seemed more than enough before, but was now cramped because she had spent one day in the king's palace. She had said she would take a week to think about it, but how could she and Atir make a real life here, with her mother so needy? And what about when they had children?

13

Abish prayed every night during that week for an answer about the king's offer. She had begun to think once more about the vision she'd had about her mission to save her people.

One night Atir caught her praying. "If you must worship the Nephite god, you should do it in silence. What if anyone were to hear you? We could both be killed if they think of you as a Nephite spy."

"I have to be true to what I know is right," Abish said.

Atir thought a moment. "This is the reason that you didn't want to accept the king's offer, isn't it?" he said. "You're afraid of the consequences if you're caught praying to the Nephite God in the palace itself."

"No, that isn't it," Abish said. But perhaps it should have been. Could she simply stop praying? Or pray only in silence?

"King Lamoni is a good man, but he could not forgive you for that," Atir said. "We will stay here." He nodded at the meager home she and her mother had shared for so long.

Abish took a deep breath, and knew that it was time to explain everything to Atir. Perhaps she should have told him before now, before they were married, but she had at least given him a hint. Now Abish more fully explained about her father's vision when she was born, and about the vision she herself had had when she saw her own mission laid about before her and felt the love of the One True God.

Atir shook his head with each new part, and then he put out his hands in a firm gesture of ending. "I can't allow any of this anymore. You are my wife now. It is my responsibility to keep you safe. My history with the Nephites only makes this more dangerous for both of us. You must keep quiet about all of this. You must never speak of it again, and you must pray to the Lamanite gods like everyone else. It is the only thing that will keep us and our family safe here."

It was a reasonable thing for a husband to say. He was the head of her household now, the future father of her children. But Abish felt a burning in her heart and knew that she could not stop praying. The love of the One True God had made it possible for her to survive through all the years of poverty and deprivation she had endured. She could not abandon Him now when it was convenient.

"Please, pray about it yourself," Abish said. "Pray to the One True God, and see if He answers you. Please, Atir, this is the only thing I will ever ask of you, I swear it. Pray sincerely and with a humble heart. He will answer you, or if He does not, I will have my own answer."

Atir did not make any promises, but Abish continued to pray and hope.

At the end of the week, Atir woke up before he went to give her answer to the king. "I have had a dream," he said. "A vision."

Abish reached for his hand and in that moment, she felt a warmth and joy she never had before. This went beyond her own knowledge of the love of the One True God. Her husband believed her. He shared her faith. She could never fear anything after this. So long as she had Atir at her side she could face any deprivation, any threat.

"I saw you," Atir said, "as a baby. I saw your father holding you in his arms, a look of anger on his face. And then he was bathed in a white light, above all other light. It was pure and washed him clean in its whiteness. When the light went away he was completely changed. He was the man I knew him as, the kind and gentle seeker, the man who was always honest with his workers, always trying to do better for everyone around him."

"I only ever knew my father that way, but my mother remembered both versions of him. She saw how the Nephite God changed him," Abish said.

"And then I saw you as a little girl, growing up as if protected from all sides. I saw you lifted away from a rabid animal that might have bitten you. I saw you saved from a falling wall at your father's business. And men who might have hurt you in the streets were led away. The Nephite God has chosen you because you are meant to do something great and marvelous in the future." Atir looked at her with an awe she had never seen before.

Abish felt both blessed and uncomfortable at this. It wasn't that she had been born superior to anyone else. She was no better than her sisters, and they were no better than others in the city. She had been a beggar and had seen that there were other beggars who were no less intelligent or hard-working than she was. But she had been preserved for a special purpose. It was a burden on her because she knew that she had a responsibility to her people. She could not turn her back on her purpose. She owed them for her very life.

Atir went on, staring at her. He spoke slowly, as if the words were coming to him one by one. "Your purpose is still unfulfilled. There is an emptiness in you. The Nephite God is waiting for you to do more."

"Yes," Abish said. That was it. Atir understood.

He bowed his head. "I feel blessed that I was allowed to marry you. I do not know the Nephite God well. But I know that He has great power, and I know that He must trust me to be with you."

"You are a good man. The best of men," Abish said. She thought of the men her sisters had married and knew she had been led to Atir by the One True God. "I wouldn't have married you if I wasn't sure you were the man that He wished me to be with."

"What? You were not so desperate you would have married any man who offered?" Atir said, teasing.

Abish shook her head solemnly. "As I vowed to my father I would never marry. I didn't trust men then. I thought they would all be like Laman." She hadn't even conceived of a man like Jakob then. She'd thought Laman was as bad as it could be.

"What changed your mind?"

"You changed my mind," Abish said. And the Nephite God. It hadn't been poverty or desperation. She could have survived on her own for the rest of her life if she had needed to. She had kept herself and her mother in a shelter with enough food for years. She could have continued.

"I haven't finished," Atir said after a moment. "There was more to my vision."

Abish was astonished. "Then tell me," she urged him. She'd seen her own vision of the future, but now she was anxious to know if Atir had seen more than she had. She still didn't know how she was to save her people. She was no princess. She wasn't even her father's daughter anymore. The most she could see was to be the king's servant, and that seemed a lowly place for a savior to begin.

"I saw you working in the palace. You wore no jewels, no expensive clothing. You had sweat on your brow. You were calling out for help, but there was urgency in your manner. Then I saw the king, on the floor beside you. He looked dead. His eyes were closed, and he was not moving."

"What?" This was new information, but it didn't help her at all. If the king died while she was with him would she be blamed for his fate? How would that lead to her saving the Lamanites?

"He looked hardly older than he is now, Abish." Now Atir sounded afraid. "I thought that it could happen tomorrow. You looked the same age you are now, as well."

"But how can that help anyone? If the king dies, his oldest son is still too young to take the kingdom." In a Lamanite kingdom, the man who proved himself most capable took the kingdom at the king's death, and it was only sometimes the king's eldest son.

"I don't know. The Nephite God didn't show me that part. Only that you were near the king when he fell dead. There was a light around you again, and I could see the love of God in your eyes. You were not afraid. You were sure of yourself, and it was as if you looked up into the heavens and whispered to God that you would do what you were meant to do."

Abish shook at this, and Atir held her in her arms, rubbing her shoulders to try to warm her.

"We must not speak of this to anyone," he said. "It is still very dangerous. Until the moment that you see the king dead, we must be silent except when we are at home and safe."

Abish wished that the Nephite God would give her more information. Why couldn't these visions be more clear? Or was it possible that they had been clear in the moment, and she and Atir and her father simply did not remember them well enough?

"This isn't what I would have chosen for my life," Abish said.

"You mean you would have preferred to remain your father's princess and never marry?" Atir asked. There was both humor and seriousness in his tone.

The truth was, Abish wouldn't go back to being her father's princess. Oh, she wished he were still alive. But she couldn't wish away the lessons she'd learned from living on the street. She was glad she had learned more compassion, and she wasn't sure she could have learned it any other way. She was also glad that she'd learned how to survive on her own. She had a confidence now that she'd never had before. She had courage too.

If her father hadn't died, she couldn't see how she would have found Atir, either. She might have met him, but she wouldn't have considered him a man to marry. She wasn't sure she would ever have changed her mind about marrying if she hadn't learned to look further than a man's purse.

She could see now the beginnings of the shape of a plan that the Nephite God must see in its entirety. But it might not have made sense to her if she had seen it before. It might have been a bright light she had to shield her eyes away from. It might have seemed too much like a curse to be grateful for.

"I'm glad that I found you," she said to Atir.

"What do you think your life would have been like if your father had not died?" he asked.

Was he curious or was it more than that? "I might never have married as I vowed," she said honestly. "I would have lived with my parents until they died, and then I would have tried to run my father's business. I would have ruled them all with an iron fist." She smiled at this, but it was painful to think that she might have been more like Jakob than was comfortable.

"And then? No marriage, no children?"

"I think I would have been an auntie who spoiled her nieces and nephews," Abish said. She could have helped Nesha and Tamar if they had allowed it.

"But you would never had your own daughters and sons? What a loss to the world," Atir said, making a face.

"You think I will be a good mother?" Abish said, leaning into Atir and giving him a kiss.

"You will be the best mother any child has ever had. I'm half envious of our children to be." He beamed at her.

"How many will we have?" Abish asked. "Did you see that in the vision?"

Atir's face fell. "No," he said. "I didn't."

But that meant nothing. She would have children.

Abish told Atir to tell King Lamoni that she would serve him, but that she would remain in her own home, such as it was. Then she could continue to pray there without worrying if she would be overheard and reported on to the king.

The next week she went to the palace and entered with the other servants. She was first given a position in the kitchen. Like any servant, she would have to work her way up to more trusted positions. She did not mind the work, though it was hot and back-breaking, and she went home every night exhausted to try to help her mother, who was becoming more and more feeble.

Abish tried to keep telling herself this would all be worth it. This was the beginning of a wonderful story that would end with her saving the kingdom. But cleaning out the ovens of crusted blood did not seem very miraculous. And she never saw the king, looking near death or otherwise. She never saw any of the royal family, except from a great distance. She had no idea if she was helping the young princesses learn anything at all, so far.

Worst of all was the sadness she carried each month when she began to bleed and knew that she would not be a mother this time.

For five years she was barren. She went to healers to ask their opinion. She paid for remedies and potions. She tried this time of month and that position, and she prayed every day. She prayed only to the Nephite God, not to any of the Lamanite gods, no matter what the other servants said she should do. She prayed for a child, son or daughter, any child at all. But her prayers were unanswered. It felt as if the heavens themselves had closed on her, as if the visions had been a joke or a mistake, as if she would never again feel that warmth of love from the One True God.

And then her mother died, and Abish wept and buried her herself. None of her sisters came because the king did not force them to come. Abish felt very alone. Atir traveled often and seemed to come to her bed less often now that it always seemed to end in heartache. But the home was so empty and silent, except when filled with Abish's tears.

14

Abish learned to stop weeping that she had no children. She still found it difficult to spend time with her sisters' new children, or with any women in the king's palace who had a newborn. Older children were less difficult for her; they reminded her less of what she was missing.

She knew her life was a good one. She had a husband who loved her, even if he was not at home as often as she liked. She had contact with the princesses now, but mostly cleaned and ran errands. Then she came home a little less tired than she once had. She was safe in her position in the palace, even if she had never become a particular favorite of anyone in the royal family. She was never hungry or afraid.

She had enough to share with others and to enjoy the pleasure in their faces when she offered them a coin or a meal and stayed for a while to share stories with them. The poor of the streets had become a kind of family to her. She learned their names and their pasts. When she could, she helped them find positions with sellers in the marketplace and even, occasionally, at the palace itself.

She told herself that Atir's vision must be wrong. Visions, if they came true, often turned out to mean something very different than they seemed to mean at first. The king Atir had seen fallen as if dead might be one of the king's sons instead. Or maybe it meant something else entirely that would make sense to her in the future.

She was not a princess. She was not a shaman. She had no reason to think that she was special in any way. She was not like the stories of those who had been chosen, like Laman and Lemuel, who were stronger and faster than others their age, who were fiercer warriors and had therefore conquered their weaker brothers and set up a civilization that would last forever.

She was nothing like those who were chosen by the Lamanite gods, the children who were the most beautiful, the most graceful, or the cleverest. She had not been sent on a spirit journey to test herself. She was simply a young woman who had weathered some bad luck and become an ordinary servant in an ordinary world, married to an ordinary man, living in an ordinary house.

And then Ammon came.

She didn't know his name then, only that he was a Nephite. That was obvious from the first moment he arrived in the palace, where he was brought to see the king. He was light-skinned with light eyes and that look that Nephites had: high cheekbones and a straight, aquiline nose. He was handsome and young with the kinds of heavy muscles that only men who worked in the fields usually had.

When Abish first caught sight of him, he was shirtless and glistening with sweat. He did not seem shy about showing his body off like that, though certainly the king's daughters were ogling him as Abish had only ever before seen men ogle women in the marketplace. She was surprised the princesses didn't go up and put their hands all over his body to see if he was a flesh-colored statue or a real man.

The men who had brought Ammon in were calling for the king to put him to death. "He's a Nephite spy!" they called out.

Abish felt a shiver run down her spine at that phrase, which she had been afraid for so long would be used against her or Atir. She had no place in the throne room where the king sat in judgment on prisoners, but she edged her way close enough to the doorway that she could hear what was being said as she pretended to clean the wall and the table—over and over again.

"Quiet!" King Lamoni commanded.

It was immediately quiet.

Abish peeked at the king and saw that he was still dark-haired. He still looked young, as young as he had when she had first started working for him years ago.

"You there! Tell me how you came across this man!" he pointed at the Nephite.

"King, he was coming from the Nephite lands, walking directly into our city. I knew him as a Nephite immediately, and I called to the others to stop him and bring him to you," one of the men said, this one with a broken nose.

The king pointed at another of the men who had come with the Nephite, one with the ritualized scars of the warrior god on his chest. "Is this true?"

He flexed his chest muscles, but he was no match for the Nephite, Abish thought. He said, "Yes, King. That is just what happened. He is a spy, clearly. He came to find out all about us and go back to the Nephites to tell them our secrets so that they can defeat us in war."

There was deafening noise in the throne room then, everyone started arguing with everyone else about what should be done with the Nephite. Torture, execution by sword, dismemberment.

King Lamoni shouted it down. He turned to the broken-nose man. "Was the Nephite carrying a sword when he entered the kingdom?" he asked.

A brief hesitation, and then he admitted, "No, King."

"Was he carrying a scimitar? Any weapon at all?" the king pressed.

"No, King." His head bowed.

"Was he disguised in any way? So that he would look like a Lamanite when he came among us?" the king asked.

"No, King," came the answer.

"Then he is not a very good spy, is he?" the king said.

A few voices laughed, but mostly they seemed confused.

Abish smiled a little.

The king turned to the Nephite himself now. "You. Speak. Why did you come here?"

"King Lamoni, my name is Ammon," said the man in a smooth, even voice that made Abish want to trust him, though she hardly knew him. "And I am here to become your servant. I desire only to get to know your people better so that I can understand you."

"So that he can spy on us and defeat us in war!" insisted the first man, spitting into Ammon's face directly.

Ammon did not even bother to wipe off the spittle, but allowed it to drip down his chin and onto his chest.

"Quiet!" the king said sharply. "I did not give you permission to speak. If you speak again without my permission, it is you who will be treated as a spy for the Nephites."

That silenced the man with the broken nose.

King Lamoni turned back to Ammon and stared at him for a long moment before saying, "Why did you come to us to be a servant? Why not stay with your own people?"

Ammon did not bow to the king, but he held out his hands in a gesture of submission. "I have heard many tales of the bravery of the Lamanites. I know that our peoples have often warred with each other, but I wish to bring peace to all sides."

There were murmurs about this through the throne room, but no one dared to speak out.

"You think your flattery will save your life?" asked the king. "Why are you truly here?"

Ammon let out a long breath. Finally, he admitted, "I did many evil things among my own people. When I saw my own sins clearly, I knew that I needed to prove to myself that I had changed. That is why I say I wish to be your servant. To prove that I am changed. And if I can do anything to help both my people and yours, I will do it gladly."

Abish was so impressed with this speech of Ammon's that she wanted to find Atir immediately and ask him if he had heard anything about the man or what he had done among the Nephites. But she dared not leave. She had to hear more.

"I believe you speak truly," the king said, nodding thoughtfully. "No man comes among his enemies without weapons unless there is something extraordinary about him. You do not fear us because you have already faced your worst enemy, and that is yourself."

Ammon murmured agreement and Abish thought she could see a flicker of fear in him, but it vanished quickly.

"And so I welcome you to our land." King Lamoni turned to the others in the room and proclaimed, "This man will be treated as my guest. No one will hurt him or show him less than the perfect courtesy. He is to be set free to walk among us and treated as my own adopted son."

There were more murmurs now. The king let them go on for a time, then tapped his rod on the floor. "And to show how much I honor you, I offer you my oldest daughter to wed," he said.

The princess in question blushed briefly a nd t hen seemed pleased with this turn of events. She stepped forward. "Father," she said.

"This is Hettel," King Lamoni said, as his daughter appraised Ammon's physical attributes frankly. "You have been honest and forthright even when your life was in danger. As a reward, Hettel will be your wife, and you will raise your children here in this palace. Then you will become a Lamanite in truth, and no one will be able to say that you are a spy who intends to return to the Nephites to teach them to war against us."

Abish could see the regret in Ammon's eyes. But what a fool he was if he refused the king. It would only anger the man and hurt his pride. This was a generous offer, and beyond that, it was a way to protect Ammon if he truly wished to stay among the Lamanites.

Ammon bowed his head again and said, "I thank you, king. You are very kind, as kind as I have heard your own people say of you, and kinder than any Nephite would treat me. But I cannot accept your daughter as my wife. I have not come to be your son but to be your servant."

Abish held her breath for a long moment, waiting to see what the king's response would be.

It seemed like the whole court was waiting.

Instead of roaring in anger and embarrassment, the king clapped his hands and commanded one of his servants to bring Ammon food and drink. "If you wish to be a servant, a servant you will be. You must drink and eat first, and then you will go back into the fields to work with the sheep."

"As you command it, King Lamoni," Ammon said with another bow.

In a few moments, Ammon had dressed and left the throne room. The king sat on his throne for some time afterward, ignoring any questions asked to him, lost in his own thoughts.

Was this the moment that Abish had been waiting her whole life for? His eyes were sometimes closed, and he was still upright, not fallen to the ground. Was she to do something? She did not know. There was no spiritual feeling to press her forward, so she stayed where she was and assured herself that the king was not on the floor and did not look like he was dead. Surely this was not the right moment for her to save her people.

Rumors spread quickly about Ammon. The king's daughter said that he must be a man who liked other men, but others said that she could say nothing else. Did anyone expect that she would admit she was not beautiful enough to tempt a Nephite?

Abish heard that King Lamoni had sent Ammon to be a shepherd because he knew that there were thieves who had come many times already and stolen the king's sheep. He had threatened the shepherds that if it happened again, and if they did not protect the sheep at the price of their own lives, those lives would be forfeit.

Poor Ammon, sent into a trap he knew nothing about.

That night, her stomach churning, Abish wondered again and again if she should have done something to protect Ammon. Should she have suggested that the king might take another palace servant? Had the Nephite God expected her to do something to protect Ammon from the thieves of the king's sheep?

But days passed, and the rumors about the Nephite spy quieted down. He seemed to seemed to have fit right in to the role of shepherd.

At last, Atir came home from his long trip for the king. He had heard the rumors of Ammon even before he came to their house that night. "Is he as handsome and strong as they say?" he asked teasingly.

"If not more so," Abish said with a smile. No one would ever be as handsome to her as Atir was.

"And the king truly offered Hettel as a wife?"

"He did," Abish said, though she suspected that the king would have offered Roma, his second oldest daughter, if he'd wanted Ammon to marry his favorite.

"But the Nephite wanted only to be a servant? How strange."

"Did you hear anything from the Nephites about one of their own who had committed some great sin? Who was thrown out from their midst, perhaps?" Abish thought there must be more to the story than Ammon had explained to the king.

"A great sin," Atir said softly.

"You do know something, then!" Abish said. "Who is he?"

"One of the sons of Mosiah," Atir said, more as a question than a statement.

"Who are they? Who is Mosiah?" Abish asked, because she knew nothing about the Nephites.

Atir explained, "Mosiah was the king of the Nephites until he died some years ago. But when he died, they created a judgeship to lead the Nephite people. The people vote for the judge, and there is no more king."

This seemed very foreign to Abish. "But they do not call him a king?" Why would the Nephites make their own leadership so confusing? People needed a king to keep them strong.

Atir shook his head. "The son of a judge has no special standing. He is as likely to be a new judge as anyone else is. There is no sense of royal blood with judges."

Abish pondered this. So the Nephite who was now a servent to the Lamanite king was a son of the last Nephite king? And he had refused to marry Hettel and become the king's own adopted son? Why?

Atir continued, "The sons of Mosiah were men who went against their father, and against the chief priest of the Nephite religion. I heard that something happened to them. Some miraculous . . ." his voice trailed off.

"What, Atir?" Abish pressed him.

"A vision, I think it was. They saw a vision of their true place in the eyes of the Nephite God. They saw their own insignificance and their own guilt in doing wrong. And after that, they changed their ways and tried to repent." His tone was half-admiring, half-confused.

"And this Ammon is one of them?" Abish asked.

"I remember that name, yes," Atir said. He stared at Abish. "Should we tell the king?"

Did it matter? It did not make Ammon a spy. Abish shook her head. "Let's keep it to ourselves for now."

There was danger in that choice, but Abish felt that Ammon also had a mission and that it was part of her purpose to make sure that he fulfilled it. Perhaps, in doing that, she could also finally do what she was meant to do, though she still could not see how.

15

The next day, at the palace, Abish heard the whispered story of Ammon's inevitable battle with the sheep thieves at the waters of Sebus, how he cut off their arms and chased them away, and how he then brought the arms back to show to the king in the throne room. She could smell the scent of blood and death all through the palace, but the king insisted on a celebration. There was loud music everywhere, and the kitchens were commanded to prepare a feast.

As she helped to bring in food, Abish passed by Ammon and he caught her arm. "You were here before, looking in," he said.

She kept her head down, embarrassed at his attention. "Please, let me go."

"I saw something in your eyes. You know the truth, don't you?" asked Ammon. "You know the One True God. He has spoken to you."

"I know nothing," Abish said, and she pulled away, terrified that she would be linked to Ammon and seen as a spy.

Ammon let her go, and he did not call her out publicly or even look at her during the celebration.

After the feasting King Lamoni called each of the shepherds to report on what they had seen and what Ammon had done.

Each man told the same story. Ammon had defended the king's sheep valiantly and had never seemed to be afraid of the thieves.

"He said that God would protect him. Each time he cut off an arm he whispered a prayer. I heard it," said one of the men.

Abish froze, worried that the king would ask next what God Ammon had prayed to, and then the truth about Ammon's Nephite beliefs would come out.

But the king looked at Ammon and said, "They say that the gods come among us themselves at times, to show us their true faces."

Ammon was humble, and yet he did not simply say what the king wanted to hear. He said, "It is true that the Nephites believe that there is One True God and that He will come to His people in the fullness of times and reveal Himself to them, though He will be veiled in flesh and will appear as one of them."

"The One True God will have flesh?" echoed King Lamoni in surprise.

Abish was holding so tightly to the dish in her hands that it broke. She had to scramble to pick up the pieces, but she dared not leave the room. She had to hear the rest of this. She had to know what would happen to Ammon. If he admitted belief in the Nephite God here, in the king's palace, and lived, did that mean that she could speak openly of her beliefs and not fear being put to death?

"We don't believe in many gods, but only in one great God above all," Ammon said.

There was no fear in his voice. Abish could admire him for that. His held his head high. He would not apologize for his God. Abish admired him immensely for that.

"And this Great Spirit will be the one who comes down in flesh and lives as a man?" asked the king.

"Yes," Ammon said.

"He will pretend to be one of us, but He will have power that proves that He is greater than any man could be?" asked the king.

"Yes, He will do many miracles and call His people to repent and return to the One True God," Ammon said.

Abish realized what King Lamoni believed before Ammon did. The king was staring at Ammon intently, with the kind of awe that was reserved for worshiping at the site of an earthquake or a hurricane or one of the other proofs of the touch of the gods in the Lamanite world. The king thought that Ammon himself was this Great Spirit. He thought that Ammon was the One True God veiled in flesh.

King Lamoni turned to the other men. "Do you think that any mere mortal could have done what this man did? Slaying so many of the enemies of the king and taking no injury himself?" he asked.

Now the court began to be filled with murmurs, and Abish saw many of those who had watched Ammon with interest begin to edge away from him. They had become afraid, either of his power, or of what the king would do to a blasphemer who suggested that he was one of the gods and above even the king himself.

"I do not know if he is the Great Spirit," said the one of the shepherds who still stood next to Ammon. "But I know that he could not be slain by the enemies of the king. I also know that he is a friend to the king, for why else would he use his power to save the king's sheep and the king's servants?"

Clearly, the man had bonded with Ammon in the fields and was not going to allow anything to happen to him if he could help it. Abish was impressed that Ammon had won such loyalty so quickly from a Lamanite who had worked with him as a shepherd.

King Lamoni stood up from his throne and approached Ammon.

The court grew hushed. The king was holding his sword out. Was he going to kill Ammon?

Abish looked again and saw no sign of fear in Ammon. He was not sweating. He was not shaking. He did not look away from the king. He was at peace.

But instead of using the sword on Ammon's form, the king dropped it in front of him and then bowed before Ammon. "I know now that you are the Great Spirit," he said in a formal tone. He waved at the court around him to follow suit, and soon everyone was bowing, everyone but Abish, who was still in the corner.

Why should she bow? Ammon was only a man. He was not a God. Everyone had misunderstood what he had said.

Ammon put a hand out to the king and said, "Behold, I am a man as you are. I am not the One True God of whom I have spoken. I am not the one who has taken on flesh to show Himself to His people. I am only a servant of His, as I am a servant of yours."

King Lamoni did not speak for some time after this, staring at Ammon as if he worried this was a test.

But Ammon bent down and put the sword back in the king's hands. "Truly, I am a man. I am a Nephite. I am no more a God than you are."

The king's face was flushed, but he stood. "How do you know what I am thinking?" he demanded. "If you are not a God yourself, how did you know what to say to me to allow a Nephite to come into my palace and not be killed?"

"I listened to the voice of the God as He spoke into my heart the things to say to you," Ammon said.

"And what about the men you slaughtered today in the fields? How did you have the power to kill so many? Surely that is not the power of a mortal man alone," the king said. His voice was stuttering and fearful. Abish had never heard the king like this, so unsure of himself.

With a wave of his hand at the heavens above, Ammon said, "That power was also from the One True God of the Nephites. He helped my sword arm and protected me, as He has always done for those He chooses to be His servants. There are many stories among the Nephites about our ancestors—Noah, who built a ship before the great flood, and Moses, who opened the Red Sea so that His people could walk to safety from the Pharoah, and many, many others."

King Lamoni was speechless. Abish suspected that he knew as little of these stories as she did, but she had a burning in her bosom that made her certain that they were real. The Nephite God was testifying of the truth of Ammon's words to her. She wished that she knew more of these people, but she'd never been allowed to ask about them or read about them.

The Lamanites did not have the records that the Nephites did. Some Lamanites said that the Nephites had stolen many things in the old days, before they had separated from each other and become enemies. But Abish had never known what these things were. No wonder the Lamanites could not worship the One True God and had learned instead to worship the gods of the land and the sky. They had no way to know who the True God was.

"This God of yours gave you strength to kill dozens of men? And He told you what was in the heart of another man?" the king said. "If so, then I would like to know more of Him from you. How can I get this power, and how can I give it to my men? If we had such power we would be an unstoppable army."

Did Ammon understand what the king was saying? If Ammon told his secrets, the king seemed to think that he would be able to defeat the Nephites. Surely that was not what Ammon wanted. He had come, he said, to bring peace—to save souls, not to win wars.

"I can tell you about the One True God," Ammon said, "if you would like to hear of Him. But He is not a God of war or of power. He is a God of love, and He desires only that His children hear of His love and come to know Him. He desires that all come to Him so that they will have eternal life with Him."

"Eternal life? What is this?" asked King Lamoni.

"Eternal life is life in exalted form, as we are now, but perfected." Ammon pointed at himself, his own body. "We will live with God in a better world, and we will be forever with those we have loved here, our parents, our children, and our most beloved wives or husbands."

The king gasped at this and finally said, "But not one of the gods of the Lamanites offers the chance to live again with those we love here. Truly your God is the greatest of all the gods."

Abish thought of her vision of the other world and her knowledge that her father was there, waiting for her, as was her mother now. Families were meant to be together there, forever. That was the promise that Ammon was offering from his God, and she knew that it was true.

What Ammon did not know was that King Lamoni had lost his eldest child, a son. It was not well known in the kingdom, for the king did not want others to think him weak. And Queen Amar herself had been ashamed of what had happened, though as far as Abish could tell there had been no fault in it. She had many other children and had been strong enough to deliver all of them. Only her first son had been born dead, after many hours of labor.

Abish herself had heard of this only through the queen herself, who had been weeping one day when Abish found her. She admitted that she wished she had been able to name her son and to know him before he died. His loss was greater than anything else in her life—the idea that he was gone forever, that the gods had taken him and remade him into something else that she would never know.

"Our God loves us as His children. He has sent us here in families so that we can feel that love, and when we die we return to Him as loving families, to live forever with Him and to learn to become more like Him," Ammon said.

King Lamoni began to tremble now and looked about the room for the queen. She was across the way, but their eyes met, and Abish could almost see the message passing between them: we must listen to this man.

"I will believe anything that you tell me about this God of yours and how to make myself one of His children," the king said, his voice hardly more than a whisper.

"If you listen to my words you will know all that I know of the One True God and of His love for you and for all people," Ammon said.

But Abish thought to herself that the king was already a child of God. Nothing Ammon did could make him more or less beloved. That was why she had worshiped the One True God in her heart from the beginning. That was how the Nephite God differed from the Lamanite gods. The Lamanite gods demanded prayers and attention, or they would not favor you. But the Nephite God was not like that. He did not ask for anything but for His people to be happy and to show love to others as He showed love to them. This was the greatest God, but perhaps Ammon did not understand the difference, and that was why he didn't explain it to the king.

"I will listen to your words and do all that you say. Whatever I must do to worship this Great Spirit of yours, I will do it," King Lamoni vowed. "And I will cause that all my people will do the same."

Ammon began teaching the king very simply, step by step, about the One True God. He explained that God had created the earth and the heavens, that He was all-knowing and all-seeing and all-powerful. "He created the mountains and the valleys, the sun and the stars and the moon. He created the rivers and streams, the oceans and the rain. He created all creatures, from the birds to the worms, from the bears and leopards to cattle and humans and all things below us."

This was more than a combination of all of the Lamanite gods, for though they had separate spheres, they were not all-knowing or all-powerful. Many of them cared very little for human concerns and did not think of humans as part of their family.

"A portion of God's Great Spirit dwells in me so that I can hear His word when He speaks," Ammon continued. He told the stories of the Nephite tradition, the first man and woman on the earth, the great flood and the prophet whose family survived it, about the time of slavery in another country, about Lehi and his vision of the destruction of the great city Jerusalem, and all that had happened since they had come to the new land—the wars and destructions between the people.

Abish felt faint after all of this. She did not know how many hours had passed, but she was sure that it was near dark by now. And yet the king had not called for a rest or for food to be brought to them to relieve their hunger. No one else in the court dared to suggest it either. Some of them were as rapt as the king was, listening to Ammon, but not all of them were.

Finally, Ammon began to explain about the coming of the One True God in human form, which he said that all of the prophets of God had been declaring to His children from the beginning of time, from the first man and woman, until now. He said that God would become a little child and would grow as a man would, but with power and glory and great love. And He declared to the king and the whole court that this man would make a great sacrifice for all, and that by this sacrifice everybody's sins could be forgiven and wiped clean. He said that God would die and raise Himself up again on the third day, so that all could know that there was no more death, that God had banished the end of life so that all might live together in perfect love and harmony.

"This God will come to visit us here, as well, after He shows Himself to His own people. He will visit all of His children wherever they are in the world, to show His love to them and to promise them that they will one day dwell forever in His love," Ammon concluded.

"This is true?" asked King Lamoni, his voice as hoarse as if he had been the one talking all this time.

"It is true," Ammon said with that smooth voice—and a rumble of something else that Abish recognized now as the Spirit of the One True God.

The king turned to look up at the skies. "Then have mercy on me, Great God, as you have had mercy on the Nephites, and on my people."

The words were scarcely out of his mouth before his whole body shook as if in a great agony. Then he fell to the ground and looked as if he were dead.

Abish stared at the sight of the man, exactly as it had been in Atir's vision. The king's hair was still dark. He looked young, and he was unmoving. Even his chest did not seem to rise and fall with breath.

The whole court was staring at the king.

Abish worried that one of the king's advisors could seize power now and to send Ammon away, or order him killed—if he could be killed. But the queen stepped forward.

"Take my dear husband to his bed. The king must recover from this truth you have brought to him. We will allow him to rest, and then he will return and give you your answer." She spoke so regally that no one tried to stop her as she directed servants to take the king's body to his bedchamber and lay him on a bed.

But after a full day had passed and he had still not awakened, Abish heard rumors that the queen was preparing for a burial and that she was telling her children to gather their mourning clothes.

It was time for Abish to do the work she had been prepared to do since before her birth.

She had to stop this. She had to save her people. She had to tell the queen that her husband had received a vision from the One True God, and that he was still alive.

She called Atir to her that morning, and they held hands, knowing the danger that would come from this.

"Surely the queen will be glad to know that her husband is not dead," Atir said.

"Yes, but if he never wakes? What use is he to her then, or to the kingdom?" Abish said. She wanted to trust in the One True God to do all that was right, but she was afraid. She was not sure that she was equal to the faith that had been placed in her by so many.

16

That morning as Abish walked into the palace, the queen called for her.

"Is it safe to go? What does she want?" Atir asked, holding Abish back.

"I'm sure she's still worried about her husband. I must go to her," Abish said, trying to trust that all would happen as it must, and that she was prepared to do what was necessary to save her people.

"But why you, of all the servants in the palace?" Atir said.

"Because I truly love the king," Abish said, keeping her voice steady. And because the One True God had acted to make sure she was in the right place at the right time.

"I will pray for you while you are gone," Atir said, as he kissed her before she left.

The palace was busy, and Abish saw many servants moving in and out of the throne room. She felt sick at the thought of what was going on while the king was in his bed. Were his advisors already moving to take his power and make themselves kings? She did not know any of them well, but she did not believe they were the equals of the man who still lived.

Upstairs, she knocked on the door of the queen's room. There were no guards, which Abish thought strange. There were no other servants either. The queen herself opened the door and beckoned Abish within.

"My queen, what can I do for you?" Abish asked humbly with her head bowed.

"I must know if he is dead," said the queen. She waved at the still body on the bed. "Look at him for me. There are many who say that he is dead and that he stinks. My son has gone to prepare a sepulcher for him so that we can bury him, but I don't believe that he is dead."

Abish approached King Lamoni, kneeling beside his body. She could not see any rise and fall of his chest. She reached for a hand and lifted it to her face. It felt cool, but not cold.

As she bowed her head, seeking an answer in prayer, a voice spoke to her in her mind, "*He is not dead. Send for Ammon to raise him.*"

Was this her moment? She was to save her king's life, and that would be how she saved her people? Abish's heart was thundering as she got to her feet and turned to the queen. "Have you called for Ammon?" she asked.

The queen shook her head. "He is a Nephite. I don't trust him, even after he protected the king's sheep. He is not a healer or a shaman. How can he help my husband in his current state?"

"He is a man of God. Call him and your husband will rise," Abish promised.

"But what if . . ." the queen began to ask something, then bit her lip.

"You're afraid that people will say that it is not your husband, but some animal spirit that has taken his body? That a Nephite controls your husband, is that it?" Abish asked. This time there was no voice speaking to her, but she felt prompted nonetheless that this was what the queen feared. There were many stories among the Lamanites about animal spirits possessing bodies that were not their own.

"The king's advisors say that Ammon is an enemy of the kingdom. They want to kill him. They have had him detained in prison since the king fell ill. I don't know if I could get him out if I wished to."

But these advisors were all too eager for the king to be dead so they could take control of the throne.

"If I found a way to get Ammon here, would you let him see your husband?" Abish asked.

The queen hesitated for a long moment, then nodded. "It is my only hope. If I don't do something soon, they will bury him, and he will be surely dead then."

Abish left the room and hurried back to Atir. She explained what had happened with the queen. "We must find a way to free Ammon and bring him to the king," she said.

Atir took a breath and then closed his eyes. Abish could see his lips moving in silent prayer. He spent long minutes praying and was then was silent for even longer. Finally, he nodded. "I know what to do," he said.

Abish didn't ask him what it was. She simply followed him down to the prison where Ammon was being held. There were at least a dozen guards there, which Abish would have thought ridiculous for any other man. But after what Ammon had done to the men by the waters of Sebus, she could understand why the sons of the king were afraid of Ammon's strength—and of his God.

Atir turned to look at Abish. "I'm going to do something dangerous," he said. "But trust me and trust the One True God. This is His plan, not mine. He has promised me that I will be safe and that you will be able to get Ammon to the king." He stared into her eyes, and it was all she could do not to weep. She nodded.

Then Atir struck one of the guards full in the face, called him a "Nephite dog," and began to run. All of the guards chased after him. None of them noticed Abish standing to the side.

When they were gone, Abish wished that Atir had told her about the second part of the plan. How was she to get Ammon out of the prison now? She had no keys, and his cell was surely locked.

She went inside, calling his name, "Ammon? Are you here, Ammon?"

She found him, sitting calmly inside a cell, his hands folded in prayer.

"Ammon, I've come to get you out. The guards are gone," she said. She didn't mention the problem with the locked door. And indeed, it was not a problem. Ammon stood, walked to the door, and opened it as easily as he would have any other.

Had the One True God simply unlocked it? Or had the guards forgotten in their concern for other things?

"I knew you would come for me, Abish," Ammon said.

He even knew her name? Surely only the One True God could have told him that.

"Is the queen waiting?" Ammon asked.

"Yes," Abish said, nodding her head. "His advisors think he is dead, but she is sure he is still living. Can you restore him to life?"

"Only my God can do that," Ammon said. "But it is time. I will go and speak to him when he awakens so that he is not afraid of what has happened to him. I think you know what it is like for a man who sees a vision and knows that suddenly the world is no longer what he thought it was, and that he is of a far lower station than he ever imagined possible."

Ammon had received his own vision, Abish remembered from what Atir had told her. He had seen his own lowliness in comparison to God.

"Hurry," she said, but there was no need for that. Ammon's strides were long and quick, and she had to push herself to keep up with him.

Soon, they were at the door to the king's bedroom, and the queen was letting them in.

"Please," she said. "If you can save the king's life, I will give you anything, even half the kingdom."

The king had already offered Ammon his daughter, but now the queen was trying this.

"I did not come for a reward," Ammon said. "I came to show you the power of the One True God so that you would believe and be saved."

"I will do whatever you say if you can raise my husband from the dead," said the queen. Her face was blotched with tears, and her voice was raw.

"He is not dead," Ammon said. "He is having a vision from God. And he is ready to wake." Ammon raised a hand, and the king began to stir.

It was the first sign of life in him, and when the queen saw it, she let out a cry and put a hand out to steady herself against the wall. "Lamoni!" she called out.

He turned his head toward her, then lifted a hand. "Amar?" he said, his eyes fluttering.

Abish saw the way that the queen flew at her husband. There could be no doubt that these two loved each other deeply. It was not merely a show they put on for their people. No wonder the king was so touched by the promise that he would be with his family again in the other world, and that the love of God was like a father's love for his children.

"How are you feeling? Are you weak? Are you thirsty? Hungry?" She held up a cup to his mouth so that he could drink. He sipped at it.

He did not seem weak, though if he had been ill and had not drunk or eaten in the last three days, he would have been unable to stand. But he swung himself up from the bed and took to his feet.

"Wait! You must be sure—" the queen said, but the king did not need her help.

"Blessed be the name of the true God," the king said, looking at Ammon and then at the heavens above. him

Abish whispered to Ammon. "Perhaps you should leave now. You have made many enemies here. The sons of the king will wish you dead."

But Ammon shook his head. "The God of the Nephites will protect me until I have finished my work here."

The king said in a steady voice, "Thanks to you, Ammon, I have seen the One True God in His heavens. I have seen Him as He will appear to His own people in Jerusalem and as He will appear to the Lamanites and Nephites when He has risen and put on his eternal flesh."

"He comes to save us all," Ammon said humbly, though his countenance shone with glory.

The king continued with conviction. "He will lie in a tomb for three days, as I have lain near death for three days. And when He rises again, He will never die. And I know that, because I believe in Him I will also rise again. And so will all those I love."

The king held out his hands to his wife., who was weeping uncontrollably.

"We must go—to the throne room. They must see you," the queen got out. "Your advisors must know you are alive. Quickly."

Ammon and Abish followed after them. Abish worried about Atir and what the guards would do to him when they caught him. Did the king need to intervene to save her husband's life?

In the throne room, the whole court turned and gasped as one at the sight of the king. "I am well. The Nephite Ammon did nothing to me. I have been conversing with the One True God, and am here to tell you all that He is real and that we must turn to Him to be saved," the king said.

The shepherds stood and pointed at Ammon. "We told you that he is a servant of the Great Spirit!" they proclaimed.

"Not a great spirit, but our Father. And we will all be raised to eternal life through His Son, who will come to us to show Himself in love to our descendants," the king said.

Abish waited to see what the king's advisors would do. Only minutes before they had been planning which of them would take his place on the throne and what his funeral would be like for the kingdom.

But they must have truly loved King Lamoni, or felt the Great Spirit moving through them, for they all knelt down before him and called out to the One True God to ask for forgiveness for worshipping the Lamanite gods. They listened as Ammon explained about the coming of the Christ, the Redeemer, and all swore on their lives that they would follow the king and worship the One True God of the Nephites no matter what it cost them, even if it cost them their lives.

All were overcome in this moment, unable to stand. Even the king, who had seemed hale and hearty as he came into the throne room, leaned forward on the throne and could not rise. His eyes closed once more, and the queen fell down before him.

Only Ammon and Abish herself remained standing.

"Go!" Ammon said, waving at her.

And in that moment Abish knew that this was what she had been waiting for her whole life. This was her chance to save her people and bring them to the One True God.

She ran through the palace, calling for all the servants to go to the king's throne room. Then she ran to the marketplace and called for everyone there to follow her. She ran through the wealthiest streets in the city, to what had been her house once, and to Jakob's business. She ran to the river, to where the poorest of the poor lived, and then she ran back to the palace.

"King Lamoni has been saved! Come see the Nephite who has saved the king! Come hear about the One True God and His love for His people! Come hear how you can live forever with your beloved family! Come to feel the love of the God who will take on flesh and live among us!"

Her voice was hoarse by the time she returned to the palace, but there were hundreds—no, thousands of people following her. She had not realized how many there were until they streamed into the throne room, staring openly at the king and the queen and all those who were fallen before them.

"This is the proof that the Nephite God is the true God, for this Nephite came to save us and to tell us of our true place," Abish said, gesturing at Ammon.

She thought that the only danger to Ammon might be that he would be worshiped or mobbed by those who wanted to show their admiration for him.

Instead, a man stepped forward with a sword. "My brother died by the hand of this man, and now I will slay him. He is only a Nephite, and he knows nothing, about the true God or anything else." He thrust his sword toward Ammon, and Abish held her breath.

Ammon showed no sign of fear. Once again he trusted in His God. He did not even try to move to the side to evade the touch of the sword.

And he was right, for the man with the sword fell dead at his feet, the sword clattering to the floor within inches of Ammon.

"You see? This is what happens to those who try to fight against the Nephite's God and His love. He sent me to you to bring you home to him," Ammon said. "He only wants to enfold you in His arms and bring you safely to eternal life and to a place where you will be with your loved ones forever."

Abish could hear the whisperings among the Lamanites at this. Some said that this was proof that Ammon was the Great Spirit. Others said that it was proof he was a demon, sent by an angry god to bring vengeance to the king. Still others said that he was only a Nephite and that he had killed the man by a trick.

Abish went to the queen and shook her. Only the king and queen could stop the rumors flying now. "Wake. You must wake!" she urged her, and inwardly begged the One True God to wake her in this time of need.

In a moment, the queen started. "O blessed Jesus, who has saved me from an awful hell!" She stood on her own two feet and then looked around her. "Jesus is the name of the One True God," she explained to the other Lamanites. He will save us all! We will all live again with Him after this life. We only have to call on Him to ask for mercy!"

Some of her servants began to shout out the name "Jesus" as they did for their own gods, but she did not stop them.

She saw her husband and went to his side. She bent over him and took his hand.

King Lamoni rose to his feet, and when he saw that there were so many of his servants and people in his throne room and all through the palace, he commanded them that they should begin to worship the One True God, Jesus, who would come among them and save them all.

He pointed to Ammon and told them that Ammon was to be treated as the king himself, and that they should listen to his words as a command, and that all should be converted to the true religion and the true God.

17

Abish's life did not change as much as she had imagined it would after so many Lamanites joined the Nephit religion. She wasn't remembered as the servant who had brought the One True God to the kingdom. She wasn't recognized on the street or pointed out and whispered about in the palace. This was good, in a way, because although most of the Lamanites converted as King Lamoni had done himself, there were many others who hated Ammon and believed that the king had either been possessed by a demon or become feeble-minded after his many days of unconsciousness.

These people had secret meetings and discussed how to replace King Lamoni with one of his advisors who had not converted, or with one of his young sons in time, and they were known for harassing believers on the streets—and even killing them in dark corners if they could get them alone and vulnerable.

King Lamoni sent his guards out to find and punish those who were involved in such secret combinations, as he called them, but they rarely had success. Those who wanted to remain secret remained secret. And some of those killed, Abish thought, were probably part of the combination themselves, who had shown they were not reliable.

They would surely have targeted her if they'd known who she was and what she had done. But only she and Atir and the king and queen knew. And Ammon himself, of course.

King Lamoni called Abish to him shortly after he was revived and converted and said, "You should not be a servant here. I feel I should be your servant."

Abish smiled at this. "I have no royal blood, for all my father called me 'princess.'" She was content with her lot in life and her current place in the world. And the One True God knew her worth truly, and He had known what she would do to save her people.

"But it is not right that you should continue to labor for us like this. You who saved us all," the king said.

"But isn't that what the One True God says, that we should all be servants of each other? That He, too, when He comes to dwell among us, will be a servant?" Abish said in return.

"Not this kind of servant. Come, Abish, you must take a gift. Coin enough to live on for the rest of your life without working."

"And I should stay at home all day long with nothing to do? That is no gift," Abish said, who shuddered at the thought of being indolent all her days. Though perhaps this indicated how much she had changed since her early years. She'd been happy enough to have no work to do when she was a child. That was how she imagined she would live as a married woman, if she had married a man as wealthy as her father would have wanted.

"Then you should do other work. Would you like to be a companion to the queen herself in her bedchamber?" asked the king. "Or to one of the princesses?"

Abish considered this a moment. The queen already had three companions. If Abish was to take one of their places, there would surely be resentment, especially if one of them was demoted to be a mere house servant.

Abish loved the queen now more than ever, but she did not want to hurt another servant. As for the princesses, Abish thought it would hurt her too much to spend all off her days with children who would remind her so much of the daughters she had never given birth to herself.

"Thank you, but no," she said humbly.

"You will not allow me to gift you with anything or to promote you, and yet you thank me?" King Lamoni asked. He did not seem angry, however.

"I only want to serve the coming Christ," Abish said. "And the reward He offers me is far beyond any that you can give." She thought of her father then, and her mother, and her hope of seeing them again—and not just that, but being with them, hearing them laugh, knowing that they were no longer in pain.

"That is true," King Lamoni said. He paused a moment. "You have no doubt heard of my first son, the eldest, who was lost at birth."

Abish nodded. "I've heard."

"I did not want the news to come out because I feared the queen would be blamed and there would be pressure for me to set her aside and take another wife."

Abish murmured agreement to his. She understood his fear. A king did not have the same luxury as a normal man did to marry where he loved.

"But there was another reason. I loved my queen so deeply, and I feared that if I set her aside, she would not live. I could not bear the thought of being away from her for the rest of my life. I did not care then if she ever had another child. I only wanted her for my own sake. That was selfish of me."

There was clearly more to this. The king sounded ashamed of something. Abish was not sure why he wanted to confess it to her, but perhaps it was because she had just shown herself unable to be swayed by monetary rewards. She was trustworthy in a way that none of the king's other servants could ever be. Her loyalty was to the One True God and no one else.

"I made a bargain with one of the gods. The god of birth. I sacrificed a lamb to her on an altar by the river."

Abish shivered at this. She knew the altar he was talking about. She had seen it before. It was very old. It must have been made a hundred years ago or more. There were always desperate people who went to it to sacrifice whatever they could to make a bargain with one of the Lamanite gods. She didn't know how successful they were with it.

"I promised that I would sacrifice a lamb there every year if my queen remained with me. I asked for many sons and daughters, and said that I would make sure that all of them would worship at the same altar in their turn." His face was very pale now, and Abish was afraid he might faint again. And then what would happen? She did not want to repeat this story to anyone.

"I don't know what to do now. I cannot allow my chil-dren to continue to worship in that way, but I made a promise, and it pains me that I must break it," the king said.

"Do you believe that this god—or any of the other Lamanite gods—are real?" Abish asked.

King Lamoni hesitated, but eventually said, "I don't think so. Not real, living beings like the Christ."

"Then what kind of a promise is it to make, to a crea-ture that does not exist?" She did not see the problem.

165

The king let out a long sigh at that. "You see it that way? It is not a promise I need feel attached to?"

Abish shook her head. "Of course not." She was glad to have found so easy an answer to the king's question.

"Good. Good. And the altar?"

Abish did not have to think for a moment about that. "You should have it destroyed. It and all the altars in the kingdom to other gods. You cannot stop people from worshiping falsely, but you can make it clear that you will not make it easy for them."

The king smiled at this. "You see, Abish? You are far more than a servant to me now. You are my mentor in understanding the worship of the Christ. I would not have thought this was the right thing to do without talking to you."

Now Abish was nervous. "Surely it is Ammon you should consult about such things." Ammon was the one the Christ had sent to show all of them the way. He was the one who had the spirit of Christ inside of him and who was able to understand the mind of others because of it. Abish had just a single vision and a few whispers. She was not the equal of a man like Ammon.

"Yes, of course Ammon is important. He knows the One True God. But what he does not know is the Lamanites. That is why I speak to you."

Abish also suspected that the king was in such awe of Ammon that he could not bring himself to confess to such sins as he had to Abish.

"And besides, Ammon will be on his way to other kingdoms. Already he is speaking of where I think he should go next, what other kings might listen to his message as I did," the king said.

Abish knew that some of the other kings nearby were Lamoni's brothers, and one was his father, for the kingdoms had separated some years ago when they had grown too large to be under the control of one man. She did not know any of the other kings, however. Their reputations were as fierce warriors and stern men, no more than that.

"He will not stay to keep you company?" she asked.

The king shook his head. "He says that I must learn to listen to the spirit myself and that he must be on his way. He says that the Christ is pushing him to move forward with his great work of saving all the Lamanites, who are his brothers."

Ammon had only been with them for a few months. In some ways it would be easy to say goodbye to him because they were not used to him. But what would happen to the kingdom without him? Would King Lamoni remain true to his vision? It would be very easy for him to slip back into what he had been before.

At that moment Abish realized that this was her true stewardship: Ammon would leave and convert others. But Abish was here to keep the king on the true path. And it would take all of her effort. Of course, she must remain in the palace to do that. She must remain close to the king, though all of his other servants were men. She would have to find a way to speak to him always without making it obvious to others that was what she was doing. This would be a delicate process.

"There is one thing you can do for me," Abish said.

"What? Anything," the king said eagerly.

"My sisters," Abish said. She explained that she knew that Zara and Tamar were being abused by their husbands.

"What would you have me do? Have the guards arrest their husbands? Then they would be in jail, and how would that make your sisters better off?" the king said.

The idea that a woman might want to set aside a husband as the king was once urged to set aside his wife did not seem to occur to him. Abish sighed. Even that might not be what her sisters would want. They had children by these men. Their children loved their fathers. And in some way, her sisters might love their husbands.

"What if there were a place for women to go if they wished to find a healer and take a rest for a time?" Abish asked. "A place for women and children?"

The king considered this for a long moment. "I could have a house built," he said.

"It would need guards," Abish said. "And servants to prepare food."

"The palace can spare both servants and food for such women and children," the king said. He seemed to be more excited about the idea now.

"Yes, exactly," Abish said. But she was not quite satisfied for her sister's sake. She wished she could ask the king to send his guards through the city to look for Gala. And if she was not here, then what? Send them out to the rest of the kingdom and beyond? When would she be satisfied that there was nothing she could do for her sister?

"My brother-in-law Jakob worked for my father once. He promised my father that he would protect my mother and my sisters, and that, when he was gone, she would have an income from his business for the rest of her years. And that we would be able to live in the house that he had built with his own hands."

Once Abish had wanted vengeance against Jakob for what he had done. She suspected that if she asked for the king to have Jakob killed he would do it for her. He would trust her judgment over his own.

But Abish had given up wanting vengeance. How would Jakob's death bring back her mother? How would it change the life she had lived? And while she gave no credit to Jakob for what she had learned and what she had become as a result of his deeds, she also did not hate him. He was still her sister's husband.

"I want him to return the house to us and to restore it to what it once was," Abish said. "Including the little playhouse in the back which my father built for me." She did not tell the king that it was her little "castle" or that she had been a princess in it. Maybe someday she would find a little girl to adopt and share her castle with. But it seemed appropriate to restore what had been lost.

"Done," the king said.

"And one other thing," Abish said. "I want Jakob's business to be put under the control of me and my husband. He is not to be dismissed, but he will no longer be the owner."

The king looked at her strangely. "I thought you said you wanted to remain a servant here," he asked.

And her husband knew nothing of brick building. But still, Abish thought she could make Jakob change his ways if he knew that he had to get her approval in all things. "You said anything I asked for. Is this too much?" she asked the king.

"No, it is very little. But are you sure that is all you want for your brother-in-law? He sounds a man of perfidy. Has he converted? Has he shown any sign of real change?"

Abish knew that Jakob had converted to the Nephite God outwardly, but she was not sure that he had changed in any real way. Many people had simply followed the king's lead because it was advantageous for them to do so. At least for now.

"It is enough," Abish said. She was learning about the Christ, who would come and suffer for all, and not just those who were good. He would die so that all might live again, even the wicked, even those who had not accepted his name, all of the Lamanites and Nephites. If the Christ was willing to do all that for those who did not worship Him, how could she not do the same? Forgiveness and glory were due to all of the One True God's children, not because they had earned it, but because He loved them.

A few days later Abish made sure to find a moment with Ammon before he left. She wanted to tell him how grateful she was for all he had done. But once she was alone with him, she felt so awestruck that she could not express what she felt.

"Thank you," she said.

"I am but a tool in the hands of Christ. I cannot take credit for what He has chosen for me to do," Ammon said simply.

"Yes, but you—you gave up much to come here. You faced many dangers," she got out. It was hard to explain what she meant. He had come to the Lamanites, his sworn enemies. He had done so much to help her and all her people, and he had not known any of them personally.

"It doesn't matter. Once you have given your life into the care of the One True God, it does not matter what happens next. Living or dead, it is all the same. It is for the glory of God and for the spreading of His word."

This sounded very lofty, but it wasn't really what Abish had felt. Maybe God needed those like Ammon, but He also needed those like Abish, who had a more personal stake in the matter.

"You have no family? No wife or children? No mother or father at home in the Nephite lands?" Abish asked.

"My father and mother are both gone from this world and are in the hands of the One True God. I will see them again when it is time, and I have no wife or children. I did not think that I cared about such things when I was young enough to get them, and now I have other work to do." He waved an expansive hand, as if taking in all the Lamanite kingdoms. "I have brothers who are working with me in the gospel, but this is our cause. You and all the Lamanites are our family now, Abish."

This sounded sad to Abish, but all she could do was wish that someday, Ammon might find another family of his own, whether in this life or the next.

She went home to Atir that evening and held him tightly. She loved him so much. She could not imagine living a life without someone to come home to and be loved by—not as Ammon was loved by so many as the man who had brought them to the truth, but loved personally because of, and in spite of, who one was.

Some hours later, Abish woke up hungry, which surprised her. She had eaten well at the palace before she returned home. But her stomach growled, and she went to find some bread to eat. There was a piece of rich, leavened bread dotted with nuts that she had brought home with her for breakfast.

As she ate it, Atir woke and came in with her.

"Would you like some?" she asked, holding the bread out to him, though she was loath to share. She thought she could have eaten a whole loaf of her own.

"No, thank you," he said with a private smile.

"When we have the house again, I will be able to cook my own bread," she said. Jakob had acquiesced to the king's demand to return the house she had grown up in, but because it had been so badly damaged as a stable, the king had insisted that he make it as new, and that would take a few months' time.

"You think you will have time to cook with all of your other responsibilities?" Atir said. There was a glint in his eyes, as if he was having a private joke with her.

Abish did not understand. "What is it?" she asked. She didn't want to have to work around him to get him to tell her what he knew and she didn't.

"You've forgotten it, haven't you?" he said. "You've so immersed yourself in your new work for the One True God that you aren't even sad about it anymore."

Sad about what? "I wish you would just tell me."

Instead of using words, Atir leaned over and put a hand on her belly. "I noticed a few days ago, but I thought it was wishful thinking. Tonight, though, it was clear."

Abish jerked upright, surprised and not at all sure that she was happy. What if . . . ?

"You should see a midwife to be sure, of course. The queen might give you some advice on who is best," Atir went on.

How could Atir have noticed this when she had not? Was it possible that she was with child at last? She had given up hope years ago.

"Is this some reward from God?" she whispered, her eyes shimmering with tears so that she could hardly see Atir through them.

"Is your God one who would wait to give you what you have always wanted until your performed your duty to Him?" Atir asked.

Abish didn't think so. But if she'd had a child years earlier, perhaps she wouldn't have been where she needed to be to save the life of the king and the souls of the kingdom. It might not be God that had caused her not to have a child for so long, but God could use such things for good if He knew them. The One True God knew all.

She put her arms around Atir and wept with him for joy. There was in her heart the same warmth she had felt when the One True God had been with her before. There were three weeping for joy, not two only. The God was as happy for her as she could ever be. This was the God she knew to be the true one: a God who wept with her when she was sorrowful, a God who rejoiced with her when she was joyful, and a God who could use those He loved and who loved Him to fulfill His purposes for all His children, everywhere in the world.

Afterword

I suppose I should acknowledge two texts here that clearly, on a final read, had a great deal of influence on this book: *A Little Princess*, which I read a hundred times when I was in my preteens, and *Saturday's Warrior*, which influences a great deal of how Abish sees the premortal life and afterlife of the Nephite's One True God. I've worked hard at trying to create a "real" world here, inventing far more of the Lamanite world than I had to in *The Book of Laman*, because there, so much of the text talks about what is around them and here, there's only a few verses about Abish and very little about the Lamanites because The Book of Mormon is written from a Nephite point of view. You can also see here my feminist attempts, again, to prioritize a female story and not just a male story because I believe that even if the scriptures don't tell that part of the story, it is there. Women are powerful and find ways to change the world no matter how their society looks on them.

I spent some time thinking about the ways in which The Book of Mormon is damaging to the Native American worldview, re-colonizing them by telling them that they must acknowledge Christianity in order to be saved, and telling them also that their ancestors were evil and deserved to be destroyed and brought low by the European immigrants who took over what is now the United States. Do I do the same in this book by making Abish give up her gods? I hope not. I hope that what readers experience here is an Abish who has come to believe in her own self worth and her destiny as a savior of her own people, with no need for anyone from the outside to come in. I hope that I've made Ammon a little less important and Abish and her family more important, and I truly believe that God would do this, that He always make sure that we are powerful in our own redemption, whatever that redemption eventually looks like. I don't know that I believe the literal historicity of The Book of Mormon, but it has been a powerful force in my life and in the life of so many I love, and that is why I think it is worth retelling here.

A couple of other acknowledgements. Thanks to Janan Graham Russell, who has helped me to see the world more broadly, and Tinesha Capri Zandamela, who has done the same. I've named two of Abish's sister after them, Nesha and Jenan.

METTE HARRISON is the author of the Linda Wallheim mystery series with Soho Press (beginning with *The Bishop's Wife*). She has published *The Book of Laman* and *Vampires in the Temple* with BCC Press. She has also published numerous award-winning YA fantasies, including *The Princess and the Hound* and *Mira, Mirror*. She lives in Layton, Utah, is the mother of five children, holds a PhD from Princeton University in Germanic Languages and Literatures, and is an All American triathlete.

Made in the USA
Columbia, SC
29 March 2019